A sudden shudder went through the car, as if the whole weight of the train had shifted backward heavily. Then a sound like wrenching iron. I looked at Dad. His mouth was open, his eyes dark.

"Dad —" I said.

"The bridge —" he started. "Oh . . . no . . ."

The conductor hung on to the seat backs and made a sound in his throat. "We're falling!"

THE HAUNTING of Derek Stone

CITY of the DEAD

Look for these titles in
THE HAUNTING OF DEREK STONE series:

THE HAUNTING of Derek Stone

CITY of the DEAD

◀ TONY ABBOTT ▶

SCHOLASTIC INC.

NEW YORK   TORONTO   LONDON   AUCKLAND   SYDNEY
MEXICO CITY   NEW DELHI   HONG KONG   BUENOS AIRES

ISBN-13: 978-0-545-03429-6
ISBN-10: 0-545-03429-9

12 11 10 9 8 7 6 5 4 3 2 1   9 10 11 12 13 14/0

Printed in the U.S.A.   40

First printing, January 2009

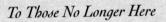

To Those No Longer Here

◄| CONTENTS |►

CITY of the DEAD

⊰ ONE ⊱

What Happened on the Train

I'll tell you straight: The dead are coming back.

You won't believe it, of course. You'll say it's crazy. It's impossible. It's whatever.

Fine. I get it. Most of the time I don't believe it myself. But it's happening, and it affects all of us.

If you're smart, you'll listen and be afraid.

If you're really smart, you'll run.

And you'll do it now, because pretty soon there won't be anywhere to run to.

I'm going to tell you everything that happened from the moment my father, my brother, and I stepped onto the train. That's probably a good place to begin. I say "probably" because I'm not sure exactly when this story did begin. Maybe it was ten years ago. Maybe it was ten thousand years ago.

But never mind that now. You need some facts.

My name is Derek Stone. I'm fourteen and just finished eighth grade. I live in New Orleans, Louisiana. I'm a little chunky. I have pimples on my chin, but not too bad. The hearing in my left ear is not good because of an infection I had when I was young. My hands are small for my age. I don't have many friends. My GPA is 4.27.

So what? So nothing. I'm telling you everything.

For years it's been just my father; my brother, Ronny; and me. Ronny is five years older than I am. We've been pretty close since he finished high school because he still lives at home. My mother left ten years ago. She said Dad was away too much, so she moved to Paris to be even farther away. Yeah, I don't get it, either.

There's one more thing you'll need to know: I don't make things up. I don't *imagine*. I don't day-dream. I like real stuff. True things. Up is up. Down is down. Fire is hot. Water is wet. I like what I can trust.

That's it, then. You know enough for me to start.

It was late afternoon on a Saturday when my dad, my brother, and I raced onto the train in Alexandria, Louisiana. Alexandria is a couple hundred miles northwest of New Orleans. We wouldn't normally be on a train, but we took one then because the day was all about trains.

My father is . . . was . . . a nut about vintage rail-road stock, the kind that rumbled through our state until about thirty years ago. North to south, east to west, they puffed black coal and white steam into the humid air. Dad loved old-fashioned locomotives. He had collected little models of them for as long as I could remember. He had tried forever to convince me and Ronny to go with him to the annual TrainMania convention. We never wanted to go, but we went this year because he really begged us and because it meant so much to him and because we were both too lazy to concoct another excuse. So fine. We went.

Imagine:

It was just after six in the evening and hot in the Third Street station, the way only a late June day could be. We flew through the gate, nearly missing the train because Dad had dawdled at the convention. He couldn't decide which of three model trains to buy, but he finally ended up with a replica of a 1928 Southern Arrow. The three of us had just jumped through the train door into the end car when the train gave a great screech. The last call for the 6:10 to New Orleans sounded over the address system.

Whistling like a kid, Dad dived into one of the two open benches and slapped the seat next to him. "Derek, here, left side. Ronny, on the aisle."

I slid between Dad and the window, with my good

ear to him. He was pumped, but I was exhausted from a full day of squeezing through aisle after aisle in a giant hall full of train geeks. For one thing, I hated the nonstop noise. For another, I was sweaty and tired. I'm not all that light on my feet, and running through the train station wasn't my idea of a good time.

Ronny sat on the aisle. Two soldiers in full fatigues took the bench seat opposite us.

Does all this matter? You decide.

Ronny and I had this gag going, which started during our race to the station. I pretended to be a cranky old man trying to get the last seat, and Ronny kept calling for "Mr. Conductor" in a British accent. We fooled around with this again until the train squealed a second time, ready to set off, and the doors started to close.

All of a sudden, a mother and daughter stumbled through the doors and stood panting in the aisle, breathless from running and clutching handfuls of shopping bags. The girl was about my age. Along with everything else, she was holding a pastry box tied with white and red string. I remember it because of what happened later.

The doors hissed shut. The train groaned a third time and began to roll. When it did, the two soldiers turned to see the girl and her mother. One of them —

a short, wiry guy with a thin face — sprang from his seat, nudging his buddy to get up, too.

"Take our seats," he said, bowing and waving his hand at the open seats.

"Please," said the other one. He was tall and had shoulders as wide as a baseball bat. As giant as he was, he had a full, round, laughing face. He looked as if he were in the middle of telling a story that he couldn't get to the end of without cracking up. "Please sit."

"Thank you," said the mother. She and her daughter sat down opposite us, while the two soldiers stood in the open area near the doors.

The moment we pulled out of the station, a block of orange light slanted between the buildings and across the girl's face. She blinked and turned her head away. I don't know if that means anything. I'm only saying that the sun was starting to set. That was some of the last of it we saw that day.

Dad unwrapped the Southern Arrow train model and studied it.

Oh, right. Here's something else. Dad loved trains, but he sold boats. He sold boats, but he didn't like the water. I guess I inherited that from him. No. That's not right. Genetics has nothing to do with it. I had a thing about water because once — no, never mind.

I'll tell you that later.

Ronny, though, was a fish. All through high school he was the best swimmer. The swim team won the state championship twice while he was captain. He must have gotten his love of water from Mom. Mom loved to swim. She swam right out of our lives ten years ago. But I already said that.

The girl's name was Abby, the girl across from us. I remember because her mother said, "Abby, can you reach up and put my bags on the upper . . . thing?"

I remember thinking she probably wanted to say "luggage rack," but couldn't think of the words.

So the girl's name was Abby. Remember that.

Dad rose from his seat to help her put the bags up.

Me, I wasn't doing anything special. I had a book in my lap, but wasn't reading it. After we settled in, Dad turned back to his miniature train and started talking about all the old stock that once crisscrossed the South. He knew a lot about them, from the Civil War on. The Del Monte, the Owl, the Golden Rocket, the Coaster, the Klamath, the Argonaut. I didn't mind listening to Dad go on. It was his day, after all. I glanced past him at Ronny, who actually asked decent questions. Dad swallowed them up, telling us everything he knew as if we'd never asked before — which we hadn't.

About an hour into the ride, when things had quieted down and I had begun my book, Abby laughed at something.

I glanced up.

Her mother was pretending to open the cheese-cake box on the sly, while Abby pretended to keep catching her.

Maybe it was the fun of the day, or maybe because the mother was acting silly, but Dad abruptly came out with: "Excuse me, ladies, it seems like you need some help with that cheesecake. Maybe I'd better hold it for you . . ."

They both looked up, astonished that we had caught them playing their little game.

"Dad!" I groaned, embarrassed.

But Abby and her mother burst into laughter. "No! No!" they chimed.

Ronny and I laughed, too.

As near as I remember, that was when Dad arched up in his seat. His eyes were fixed on something out-side the window beside me.

"What is it?" I asked, following his gaze.

"This bridge we're going to cross," he said. "It goes back to the nineteen-thirties. The Southern Arrow probably crossed it a thousand times. I have some great books about old bridges, if you guys are inter-ested. Wow, is this beautiful!"

We all looked. The bridge was a neat assembly of steel girders hatch-marked against the dark blue sky. The trestles below the tracks were pale silver, streaked with lines of rust from the bolts dotting the seams. It looked old.

We felt a bump as our car rolled across the tracks onto the bridge. The rumbling over the steel rails was loud and hollow. As the train moved over the span, the girders flashed slowly by the window to my left — light, shadow, light, shadow. The bridge curved slightly to the left, so leaning against the window I could see the engine roll onto the far side. Then the first car was on land. The second. It was strange watching the train move like a snake across the air.

As our car rolled toward the middle of the span, I saw the reason for the bridge through the trestles beneath us: a deep chasm between two steep, rocky slopes, with a dark river at the bottom. I turned away when my legs tingled uncomfortably.

"Do you have a place for the Southern Arrow in your collection?" asked Ronny, nodding at the model in Dad's lap. "In your special room?"

"All picked out," Dad said. "I'm going to —"

A sudden shudder went through the car, a feeling as if the whole weight of the train had shifted backward heavily. Then a sound like wrenching iron. I looked at Dad. His mouth was open, his eyes dark.

"Dad —" I said.

"The bridge —" he started. "Oh . . . no . . ."

The car sank, still rolling forward. Some people shouted. The conductor stumbled between the seats to the door that connected our car to the one in front of us. But our car dropped backward again. He was thrown to the floor, and we were all pushed back into our seats.

The conductor hung on to the seat backs and made a sound in his throat. "We're falling!"

◄ TWO ►

The Fall

The train car tilted suddenly to the left, setting off an alarm on the public address system.

Abby screamed. The cake slid off her lap toward Ronny's feet. Out of reflex, he lurched to catch it, missed, and fell forward almost into her. As the cake splattered onto the floor, something slammed — hard — into the roof of the car. I saw a girder twist away from the bridge and fly past the window on my left. People screamed.

I gripped my seat. Ronny struggled to stand up, then slid halfway down the aisle toward the back of the car.

"Ronny!" I shouted. It sounded like a little boy yelling, not my voice at all. "Ronny!"

"Hold on to something! Everybody!" one of the soldiers yelled, clinging to the luggage rack to hold himself up.

"Derek, grab the seat," yelled Dad, who had fallen

to the floor in the aisle. He was on his back, face red, struggling like a beetle to right himself.

Everything was tumbling toward the rear of the car.

I grabbed the underside of my seat and held tight. Abby's purse struck my face and scratched my cheek. Her mother tumbled into my seat, then flew right over my head toward the rear of the car. There was a sickening groan, then nothing.

"Mom!" Abby yelled.

Something snapped loudly, and the car fell like a dead weight. My stomach lurched to my throat. Screams echoed all around me. We saw the trestles receding above us.

We were in free-fall.

An instant later, the back end of the train struck the side of the ravine, crunching into the side of the rocks. It stuck there for a moment before flipping toward the chasm. The windows on both sides of the car exploded, spraying glass into the cabin. Suddenly, up was down and everyone slammed up to the ceiling and back again. My shoulder felt crushed. I smelled vomit.

A shaft of iron broke off from somewhere and shot through the cabin like a spear. I tried to duck out of the way, but now Dad was sprawled across my legs. I didn't know where Ronny had gone. I jammed my head down and squeezed my eyes shut. Then I felt it.

The iron shaft struck me behind the left ear like an icicle.

I blanked for a second. Warm fluid poured across my cheek, into my eyes. Ronny's hand was suddenly on my back, holding me down between the seats. He shouted in my ear, but I didn't hear what he said.

The train car stuttered down the ravine. Sparks the size of baseballs shot out the front of the cabin. I caught a glimpse of the girl, Abby, nearly upside down. She was pinned between the last row of seats and the rear door.

I couldn't believe I wasn't dead. I was still seeing things happen around me. Things I could never imagine people doing.

"Dad —" I called. "Ronny!"

The cabin suddenly surged up. The car folded onto itself, twisted backward, then buckled. One half of it ripped off and dangled on the hillside. I saw Dad slide away, down the aisle and out of sight, screaming at the top of his lungs. Our half of the car tumbled once, then stopped.

The stop was so sudden that the moment it happened — and I remember this part clearly — Ronny flew at the window next to me as if he was aiming for it. It was the strangest movement I'd ever seen.

"Derek! Derek! Help! Help —"

His mouth was wide open, but fell silent as he flew into the black chasm below.

Flame and dust clouded around me, around everything. The air was a deafening roar. It went black inside my head.

⫷ THREE ⫸

At Bordelon Gap

I was nowhere for a long time. At least, I'm told it was a long time. I don't really know.

When I finally opened my eyes, I was sprawled on the ground. It was dark except for a bright orange light flaring somewhere below me. People were screaming, crying, yelling all around. My nose stung with the smell of burning rubber.

"This one's moving," someone called out. "Frankie, he's breathing. Bring a stretcher! Medic, over here —"

Feeling came back into my limbs, and I realized I was lying on steeply sloped ground, my head toward the top of the slope. There were people and search-lights and shouting and a roaring from below. I wanted to prop myself up on my elbows, look into the chasm. When I tried, someone held me down.

"Hold on a second," said a woman. "Don't move. We have to check you over. Can you feel your legs?"

"My head hurts, my neck," I said. The pain where

the iron shaft struck me felt like a burning dagger behind my left ear. "I can't see too well."

"It's blood in your eyes," someone said.

If I'd understood, I would have been grossed out by that. But I didn't understand. Couldn't.

For the next few minutes they examined me. After they cleaned my face and eyes, my vision focused. Pain seared through my ear and into my head.

"Bruises on his face, shoulder, both knees, neck behind his left ear, possible concussion," a man said, patting a piece of gauze in a spot above my eyebrows that didn't hurt much at all. He wore rubber gloves. I smelled the latex. He pressed his fingers along my arms and legs, my stomach.

"Any of this hurt, really hurt?" he asked me.

It didn't. I shook my head.

"What's your name?" the woman asked.

"Derek," I said. "Derek Stone." My voice didn't sound like me.

"Were you traveling with anybody?"

"My father and my brother. Where's Ronny?" I croaked, trying to get up again.

"Hold on," she said, holding me down.

"Ronny! Dad!" I tried to yell, but only a hoarse whisper came out. My voice was gone. I remembered screaming all through the crash. It was catching up to me.

A loud hissing noise cut through the air as water was pumped from hoses at the fire below. At the burning railcar.

A rectangular shape swung slowly over my head, outlined by bright light.

It looked like a coffin with a halo. It was a stretcher.

"Girl, unconscious," said a technician a few feet away. "They're taking her to one of the rescue vans."

I shut my eyes to dampen the pain, then blinked them open. "The brown-haired girl?" I said, not remembering her name.

"She kept talking about 'him.' I don't know 'him,' but I guess someone helped her," he said. "She was on the edge of the ravine."

"Her mother? Is her mother okay?" I asked.

"There's someone on the rocks below," the man went on, staring into the black depths. "Somebody said they saw her, a woman."

I gazed down, squinting through the darkness. The thin strip of a river ran along the bottom of the chasm. It was black and alive, glinting silver from the lights. "Dark river," I said.

"What?" the woman asked, leaning to me.

I looked at her. "I don't know. 'Dark river, of many deaths.' That's a line, right?"

"A line of what?" she asked.

I blinked. "I don't know."

"More lights are coming soon," said a fireman, holding my arm to keep me from falling. I hadn't noticed him until then. "As far as we can tell, there are nine missing. We're doing all we can to get to them —"

"Good luck! That's the Red River down there," someone else chimed in. He had no uniform, but wore thick ropes over both shoulders and danced nervously from foot to foot. "Bordelon Gap is a hundred feet straight to the water and no more than five feet wide at the bottom. It's a sheer drop a long way . . ." He shuttled off impatiently without finishing.

"A Marine climbing crew is on its way," one of the EMS workers said to someone, not me. "They'll rappel down the ravine. The governor's called them in. We need to get these others to the hospital. Frankie, here —"

I wasn't getting it.

"Where are Ronny and Dad?" I asked, out loud this time. No one said anything.

"Put me in the same van as my brother and father," I demanded, feeling a tug at the back of my mind and hoping I would be awake to hear the response. Things got blurry.

Sirens wailed. Worse, I heard people moaning

from somewhere down the slope. Why weren't they being helped? The air stank of burned rubber, scorched oil, and a sulphurlike smell that made my eyes tear. A small army of men in jumpsuits was climbing slowly down to the edge of the ravine.

Out of the corner of my eye, I saw the water down below again, glinting in the searchlights. It was moving among the sharp rocks, always moving.

River of many deaths . . .

"It's all rocks," one of the men near me said. "We've gone over everything. I'm sorry."

"Sorry? You weren't driving the train," I said. But that wasn't what they were sorry about. It was Ronny and Dad. They weren't on the slope with me. They weren't above the ravine. They were down there. In the chasm. On the rocks. In the river. Gone.

"I'm sorry," the man said again.

The world shifted. All I wanted was for our train to be back in New Orleans.

"Come with us, up the hill," someone said gently. "Let's get you on a stretcher."

"No, no. No!"

"Come with us," someone said, sliding me onto a gurney. Two men lifted it up.

"No —" My throat filled with cotton, my head went light. I leaned over the gurney and got sick on the ground.

I had survived a horrific accident with barely a bump on my head, but my brother and my father hadn't?

They were gone?

They were dead?

◄| FOUR |►

Grief

They tell me a hospital upstate played pincushion with me for two full days. I was hooked up to a half-dozen monitors. I went through CAT scans, head-to-toe physicals, blood tests, X-rays, cardiograms. My blood pressure was monitored constantly.

I don't remember any of it.

They also tell me I called for Dad and Ronny about a million times, but I don't remember that, either.

While I was out, I kept seeing one particular moment of the crash. So many things were unclear, but I could see this perfectly.

It was when the car twisted and Ronny was thrown at the glassless window next to me. In that instant, his face filled with horror and surprise. His eyes locked with mine.

"Derek! Derek! Help! Help —"

But there was something I couldn't wrap my head around. It was the way his arms went up and out the window. They went straight out the window and then he jerked up, as if he were being pulled out of the cabin.

Pulled?

Impossible.

I began to surface on the third day of tests. The doctors were frowning, then surprised. Then they gave me more tests.

At some point, I heard that the girl — I remembered now that her name was Abby — was in a coma on another floor. She had possible brain damage and was not expected to survive.

They called her the Donner girl.

Abby Donner.

The press, I discovered, was all over the crash, hounding the survivors, haunting the hospitals. When no one could find anything more to treat, they let my dad's brother check me out. I don't know how, but Uncle Carl got me through the parking garage and into his car without running into a single reporter, photographer, or cameraman.

Carl Stone was an okay guy. He and my dad hadn't seen each other much over the last few years since Carl had moved to Oregon, where he owned a software business. But he was back, he said, for as long as I needed. That was comforting.

Around the time I left the hospital, the newspapers

discovered that this was "the second crash at the same site," and an investigation was launched into the building of the bridge. It had been built in 1936, a government project, so the investigation went nowhere except into history. Who cared about that, anyway? It made no difference now. My whole family was gone in a single evening.

Carl drove me home to New Orleans. It was a silent trip.

It was only when I saw the skyline and smelled the river that it really hit me. My brother and my father weren't going to be home as usual.

According to the media, they were "missing and presumed dead," part of a group of nine victims who were "missing and presumed dead." But you know what that means.

They were just dead.

Dad had told me it always amazed him how quickly I had understood and accepted that Mom had left us.

"France?" I had said. "That's where the Eiffel Tower is. And funny cars. Nice for Mommy." I was four.

Dad had said that on that day I had closed the hole that her departure had opened in my life. I never asked when she would be back. I understood fully that she wouldn't.

So.

Now my brother and my father were gone, too.

And I was alone.

"Here we are, Derek," Carl said, as we slowed on Royal Street. It was midday, the very end of June, and the street was as lively as ever.

"It'll get better," Carl added softly. "Day by day."

"Sure," I said.

I climbed out of the car and stood in front of my house while he parked around the corner.

My house. Right. You should know about it.

Royal Street was an ancient street and 517 was one of its oldest standing addresses, a three-hundred-year-old brick house in the heart of the French Quarter. Royal is packed with noisy jazz clubs and cafés and shops that get even noisier during tourist months. My favorite part of the house was the court-yard on the back alley. It was a jungle of plants, vines, and potted palms. It had a brick patio, two fountains, and a wrought-iron table with chairs in the center. For me, it was always one of the few places in the Quarter where you could actually relax and breathe. Noise from the street faded away when you were walled in back there among the plants.

The second story of the house was balconied over the street with a wrought-iron railing, like the grille of an antique car. At the very top stood what was called a *faux chambre*, a false room. It was shaped like a lantern, with broad windows on each of its eight sides that glared down on the streets. It sat on the roof like a pillbox, its only purpose to balance out the design of the house.

On the very tip of the roof stood a wooden figure of an angel painted gold. Wasn't there some line that went, *Angel child, child of light*? What was that from? My mind was a jumble. I turned to see the other houses on our street with false rooms. Peacocks, deer, frogs, and eagles ornamented their roofs. Dad had told me that while the room was meant just for show, he had made it into a space for his train collection and railroad books. I'd never been up there.

Carl hustled to unlock the front door, and I entered the house. Even when he dropped the keys on the table, made noise in the kitchen, and began to fix lunch, the rooms seemed strangely silent, eerie. I stood in the hallway for ten minutes without moving. I didn't know what to do. Then I went upstairs to Ronny's room.

His swimming trophies neatly lined a glass case on the wall. The rest of the room was as messy as any nineteen-year-old's room. And why not? He thought he was coming back to it.

I went to my room, collapsed on the unmade bed, and fell asleep without eating lunch.

* * *

Over the next few days, I spent a lot of time in the courtyard, doing nothing. There was nothing to say to anyone, anyway. A bridge failed, a train fell, nine people were presumed dead, and rescue workers were still searching for them. That's all. My injuries were minor, considering. The concussion from being hit in the head was the worst because of the headaches, but even those weren't so bad anymore.

A week passed and the search for survivors — and then bodies — ended. Bordelon Gap was too deep and inaccessible, the river too swift. The newspaper and TV reporters went away. There was a tornado in Kansas, an earthquake in China. The world was done with train wrecks. Everyone left us alone.

Carl decided we needed a memorial service of some kind, and that we'd do it at the family tomb. I still found it all hard to swallow. Every day, I expected Dad to call me down for dinner. Any minute, I thought Ronny would barge into my room and tell me something dumb. But I didn't like wishing for something unreal. I didn't like inventing.

Up was up. Down was down.

So on the Saturday two weeks after the crash, we went with a priest to St. Louis Cemetery Number One to say good-bye.

An aboveground warren of small stone houses, alabaster and marble and limestone, St. Louis Cemetery was divided into cramped neighborhoods, narrow streets, and blind alleys like a little city.

In fact, people called it the City of the Dead.

The day was burning hot. The air hung heavy and wet and smelling like damp stone.

Ronny's on-again, off-again girlfriend, Samantha, came with her parents. Short and blond, she had remained friends with Ronny even after their latest breakup.

After crying for a while in the hot, white sun, Sam came up to me. "Did he . . . was it painful, do you think?"

I said I didn't know. Then I remembered what one of the rescuers said. "But he was a hero," I told her. "He saved a girl. Everybody said so. She's alive because of him." I had almost convinced myself that Ronny was the "him" Abby Donner had spoken about before she went into her coma. It was probably a lie, but it hardly mattered.

Sam hung on every word. She nodded, sobbed, blew her nose, sobbed again, and left with her parents before the service was over.

Standing beside the squat white tomb, the priest began to read lots of nice-sounding words from a book, then spoke about a boy and his father. But I could barely breathe and heard almost none of what he went on about, until he mentioned "the dear brothers . . . Derek and Ronny."

Derek and Ronny.

"I miss him," I blubbered to my friend Tooley Calder, who stood next to me.

"I remember all the stuff he did to you," said Tooley quietly.

"Yeah," I said. "But I've wanted to be him forever. My whole life."

A group of mourners was assembling two streets over. I saw a trumpet flash in the sun. I expected to hear a note, but instead, there was a low mumbling sound that went up the side of my neck and behind my left ear. It felt like a needle was being pushed into my damaged eardrum.

"Don't you think?" Tooley asked.

I turned. "Sorry. What?" I said, pressing my ear closed with my finger.

"Don't you think you guys were just so different? Ronny got the brawn. You got all the rest."

I think I smiled. "But he saved that girl on the train."

"The coma girl?" Tooley asked.

I nodded.

I had come to believe my own invention, that Ronny saved Abby Donner, even though "saved" is a big word for someone in a coma. But Tooley was right, mostly. Ronny only ever turned on a computer to play a game, and he didn't know or care where the library was. He had four things in his life: swimming, girls, girls, and swimming. He was popular, thin, good-looking, social, always joking. The opposite of me.

Tooley gave me a little smile. "Makes you wonder how you guys came from the same gene pool, you know?"

I knew. But there were times when Ronny looked sideways at me with that face, the half smile lighting up his eyes as if we shared a private thing. There was something working between us.

He knew me, and I knew him.

And now there was Derek, but there was no Ronny.

Just then, someone started up some kind of grinding engine nearby. Its sound shivered through my legs and feet.

Who would do that?

Who would make that kind of noise in the middle of a funeral service?

The priest kept going as though he hadn't heard,

as though he always went on with the service no matter what. I turned in every direction, but saw no engine. It rumbled the ground under my feet and rose up into my chest.

"What is that noise?" I asked Tooley.

"Shh," he said, nodding at the priest, who was looking at me and smiling.

I returned his smile. I guess he had said my name, since others were looking at me, too.

It meant nothing.

Then the trumpet shot out a note and really did interrupt the service. Heads turned. It sounded like a dagger splitting through the air. The priest paused, then went on.

My face was draining into my chest, my stomach, my knees. Carl held me up on one side, Tooley on the other.

An hour after I kissed the tomb that contained neither Dad nor Ronny, I was finally home, feeling as dead as they were.

The next few days rolled by in a blur. I hope nothing important happened, because I don't remember much of it. What I do remember is that I met, shook hands with, was hugged by, had my cheeks pinched by, and forgot the names of dozens and dozens of family friends.

What did I care about them?

When the last person left our house, I felt like bolting the door and never leaving again. I wanted to close my eyes and see nothing.

Forget it all.

Sleep for a hundred years.

But sleep wasn't any good, either.

◄| FIVE |►

The Coming

I started to tell you before about me and water, about what happened to make me hate water more than just about anything. Sometimes I think that maybe it never really happened. That it's my own little nightmare, a horrifying memory cooked up for some reason I can't remember.

But it might as well have happened, since I'm completely terrified of dark swamps, churning rivers, and all the black watery depths that you find scattered everywhere around our ancient state.

And the dogs, of course. There are always the dogs.

The nightmare came back my first night home after the accident. And again every night after that.

Every night, the same nightmare.

And every morning, the same sickness in my stomach.

Uncle Carl did his best, but how could anyone deal with this? Even while I was in the hospital, Carl had attempted to get in touch with my mother. He'd had the U.S. Embassy try to contact her in France. There were e-mails, phone calls, cables, letters, even messengers, but she was away. No one knew exactly where. So two and a half weeks after the accident, she still didn't know. If she'd known, she would have come back — wouldn't she?

In the meantime, Carl stayed in the house with me. One day, he came out to the courtyard. As usual, I was sitting silent and alone and looking at nothing.

"Can you do your brother's room?"

That's what he said. *Do your brother's room.* I didn't understand. "Sorry?"

"Go through Ronny's room, clean it up a little?" Carl said, looking not at me, but at the bricks on the patio floor. He was holding a stack of Dad's shirts. Then his eyes met mine. "You know, it's been almost three weeks. It should be straightened up. If you think you can. Maybe pack some of his things in boxes?"

In boxes? Oh, man.

I understood. Of course, I did. But I couldn't. Messing with Ronny's stuff, the swimming trophies, the junk in his desk, his dresser, packing up his clothes, his socks? It would mean I didn't expect him to come right back.

"Can't it wait?" I said.

Carl smiled gently. "Sure. No problem. No big deal."

The way he said it made me feel ungrateful for all the time he was spending here, away from his home.

"No," I said. "It's all right. I'll do it."

He breathed in. "If you can. It might help to work through, you know, him not being here? Anyway, just a little. To start."

I did start little. I started slow. Every single thing of Ronny's, no matter how trivial, flooded me with memories of stuff we used to do together. It took me an hour to move a sock, a magazine, a CD.

Then, just before I was about to give up for the day, I heard a long, drawn-out note. A low sound, almost like the rumbling I had heard in the cemetery. In the quiet of Ronny's room, though, I heard it more clearly. It didn't sound like a machine this time.

It sounded like . . . voices. Lots of them. A chorus of voices, confused, overlapping, wild, low.

They were moaning.

I shivered, dropped my hands from the dresser knobs, and listened. I thought about the moaning at the ravine. It was louder in my left ear, the bad one, just as I'd heard it in the cemetery. I put my finger in my ear, stopped it up, then released it. The sound moved away. Turned a corner. Then it was back again, nearer. I whirled around to face the hallway. There was no one there.

Of course there was no one there.

I stepped into the hall. The sound was nearer still, but was so deep. It seemed impossible for voices to be that low. It was like something primal. Uh-huh. Right. Maybe that concussion had been worse than I'd thought.

"Who's there?" I said, intending my words to be louder.

No answer.

"Uncle Carl?" I said. That was a whisper, too. Like when I called out in my nightmare. Calling, desperate to be heard, but afraid to wake anyone. "Carl?"

No answer. I went to the landing at the top of the stairs.

"Uncle Carl?" I called down. "Are you listening to music?"

"Huh?"

I turned quickly. He was in the hall behind me. His arms were draped with my dad's neckties.

The voices softened, drew back.

"Are you listening to music?" I asked again.

He glanced behind him. "No. What do you hear?"

"Nothing," I said quickly. "Never mind."

"You all right?" Carl asked. "You know, you don't

have to do Ronny's room if you don't want to. It can wait. You look a little pale."

I was shaking all over. "I'm okay," I said.

But I wasn't okay. I was hearing things. My skull ached. Maybe I really did some kind of serious damage to my head in the accident. Maybe I'm really hurt. Maybe —

"No, I'm fine," I said, going back to Ronny's bedroom.

A little later, the phone rang. Carl was in the bathroom, and I didn't feel like answering it.

"Let it go," he called out from behind the door.

I let it go. You don't answer phones when your brother and your father die on the same day.

A second call. I sat on Ronny's bed, two feet from the phone, listening to the rings until they ended. Not long after, I heard a police siren whooping into the Quarter. I went to Ronny's window and looked down at the curb. The police car had stopped in front of my house. The whirling lights flicked off.

When the car door opened, a man climbed out of the backseat. He stepped awkwardly onto the sidewalk and stood at the curb. Then he slowly lifted his head and looked up.

My chest nearly exploded when I saw his face.

It was Ronny.

⫷ SIX ⫸

The Impossible Begins

Blood drained from my head. My knees nearly gave out.

I screamed down the stairs, tripping over my own feet, and fell flat on my face in the hall as the door cracked open.

"Ronny!"

His head poked in.

"Ronny!" I cried. He stepped in, squinting at me on the floor. I jumped up and hugged him. "Ronny! Ronny!"

I hugged my lost brother, my brother who everyone thought was dead, my brother who had gone through who-knows-what for nearly a month, and who had come back home, my brother.

But when I wrapped my arms around him, Ronny was ice cold, stiff, awkward. He felt like a tree. Wooden. Except that wood feels more alive than he did just then.

I pulled away. He looked down at me, frowning

strangely. Okay, he was in shock. Of course, he was. Think of what he'd been through!

Two police officers stood behind Ronny. One was grim-faced, somber, the other looked tired. They were both searching my face for something. I couldn't tell what.

"Come in! Oh my gosh, come in!" called Carl, practically throwing himself down the stairs. He half-laughed, half-cried. "Ronny —" His cheeks were wet with tears.

The officers stayed on the doorstep for a few minutes. They told us that Ronny had been found wandering near the ravine, had violently refused medical treatment, and had wanted only to come home. He had apparently gotten into a house somewhere and had been hiding and sleeping in the basement there for days, surviving on who-knows-what. Once the owner found out who he was, he didn't press charges.

Ronny peered past me into the house, almost like we weren't talking about him. One of the officers said that a social worker would call. Then the two men looked from one to the other as if there were more to say, but they didn't say it. Instead, they turned to leave.

"Thank you!" Carl gushed again and again as the officers climbed into their car.

We pulled Ronny inside and closed the door. He stepped back from Carl, gazing at him with a strange, distant look. He's traumatized, I told myself. Falling so far out of a crashing train. Maybe he hit his head. Maybe, in his shock, he didn't remember much. But he was home.

"You were dead," I told him, not finding the right words. "Everyone thinks you're dead, I mean. We have to tell people! How did you get out of there? How did you live through that? Where have you been?" I couldn't stop talking.

"I don't know," Ronny said, shifting nervously from foot to foot. "Just lucky, I guess. Lucky to be here." He chuckled, or tried to. It sounded like a cough. His eyes darted around, never fixing on any one thing.

This was some kind of trauma, right? Couldn't the police have insisted on medical treatment?

We took Ronny's arms and led him into the house.

"No, really," said Carl, pulling him into the kitchen. "Ronny, how did you get out of there?"

He shrugged. "I really don't know."

"Did you see Dad?" I blurted out.

He gave me a weird look. "How'd you know about him?"

"What?" I said. "What do you mean?"

"How do you know about Daddy Jubal?"

"Daddy Jubal?" I said, glancing at Carl. "Who is —"

"Right, right," Ronny said quickly. He almost looked embarrassed. "Dad. Our father. My father. Dad," he said insistently. "So he isn't here?"

Carl and I shared a look.

"The police said your father probably died in the accident," Carl said, pulling out a chair. "We don't know for sure. They haven't found any trace of him."

A worried look came over Ronny's face, starting at his forehead and sliding down to his chin.

"But they might still find him," I said. "If you made it, maybe Dad did, too."

"Oh," Ronny said. "Uh-huh, uh-huh." He didn't sit, but turned and walked out of the kitchen.

"Where is he going?" Carl whispered.

I followed Ronny. I touched his arm, but he pulled it away and climbed upstairs, leaving me at the bottom.

"He's been in an accident," said Carl.

"I know . . ." I said.

"I actually thought you'd be more like this when you came home," Carl said. "Let's give Ronny some space. And time."

Still, I followed Ronny up the stairs into his room. "Sorry for moving your stuff," I said. "I know how you like your things in certain places. We — Uncle Carl and I — didn't hear anything for a long time . . . you know . . ."

"Whatever," Ronny said coldly. He tossed a trophy onto the floor and flopped down on his bed. His eyes were blank, searching the ceiling. "Tell Momma I have to sleep. You can go now."

"Momma?"

"Whoever!" he snapped. "Don't you have mice to trap? Get out."

I stepped backward out of the room, and closed the door. Mice to trap? Something was wrong with Ronny. He was . . . changed. I don't know. I'm not telling this right.

All I knew was that something was wrong with Ronny, and it scared the life out of me.

⊸| SEVEN |⊷

The Wrong Things

At first, Ronny was all over the news.

The press had a field day with the boy who had survived the "death crash" and the "death chasm" and every other "death" thing.

But Ronny had nothing to say. Nothing. Reporters shoved microphones in his face; he shied away from them, staring at them like they were ray guns from outer space. It was clear to me and Carl that Ronny was suffering from a deep sense of shock. He couldn't find his place.

Finally, Carl closed the door on the press — shouted at them, even — and that was that.

The next few days were strained, but okay. Now that Ronny was back, Carl said he would have to be gone more during the day for business. He had visits with lawyers, probate court, and the police, plus lots of conference calls back and forth to his office in Oregon.

That was fine. I thought having the house to

ourselves might bring the old Ronny back. Things could start to be almost normal again, even though Dad wasn't there.

Normal? That's not even funny.

Carl arranged for Ronny to get back the job he'd had in high school, as an after-hours summer custodian at our old middle school. Carl thought it might help take Ronny's mind off things. Ronny agreed. His shift was 4 p.m. to 8 p.m. three days a week. He did the first shift with no problem. It was after his second shift that something happened.

I'll try to remember as many details as I can.

That evening, Carl made supper as usual. Then he went to bed early because he had to drive to the State House in Baton Rouge in the morning. I was waiting to eat with Ronny, but he didn't come at 8:30, 9, even 9:30.

I was about to wake up Carl when the phone rang. It was the head of the custodial crew at the middle school.

"Is Ronny Stone there?" he asked gruffly.

"He's not home yet," I answered.

"Well, tell him not to come back here. Ever."

"Why? What happened?" I asked.

"Because he's crazy, that's why! Setting a fire in a classroom? Look, we gave him a job because of the accident, but your brother needs help. It's all I can do to keep the assistant principal from pressing charges —"

"Fire? What?" I asked. "Can you tell me —"

"Let him tell you!"

Click.

Ronny stumbled in around ten o'clock. The first thing I noticed was the tied-up plastic bag dangling from his wrist. Something heavy pooled at the bottom of the bag. And I could smell smoke. Not cigarettes — it was something else I couldn't identify.

"Your boss called," I said, standing. "What happened?"

"I walked out," he said.

"But I thought it was working out okay," I said. "You loved that school."

"That's what the old guy said, too, but then what are these? I thought I got rid of all of them."

I took the plastic bag and looked inside.

At the bottom were what looked like rats. Three rats, maybe four, charred black. I shoved the bag back at Ronny. "Gross! Get those out of here!"

"You've seen them before," he snapped. "It was your turn last week, so these are your fault."

"What are you talking about?"

He dropped the bag on the floor. "Besides, I couldn't stand the noise in those hallways. It made my head spin."

"What noise?" I asked. "Isn't the school mostly empty in the summer?"

Ronny slapped his hands over his ears. "The voices! It was the same as at the ravine. The stupid moaning and groaning. I just want to go home. How far is it from here, anyway? I've gotta get home."

The moaning and groaning?

"Ronny, you *are* home —"

Then, I don't know what happened. He began to mutter to himself, something about a shed and a trestle and some word that sounded like "Angola." I couldn't make any sense of his words before he finally walked out of the room.

I had to get rid of the rats. I dropped them into the garbage can outside the courtyard gate and twisted the lid tight. My blood chilled.

I couldn't sleep after that. I just stared at the ceiling of my room. Rats? What exactly had Ronny done in that school? Set rats on fire?

The next morning, I found him walking down the hall to the bathroom. He opened every door on both sides of the hallway and looked in with a blank face. He left each door open and passed on to the next one, as if he were searching for something.

"Hey, you want to do something?" I asked him.

Ronny whirled to face me. "Yeah," he said, grinning

and suddenly reminding me of his face before the accident. "Maybe we can . . . maybe we can . . ."

He drifted off, his face twisted.

"Ronny?" I asked.

He turned and walked away down the hall.

"Want to go get some comic books?" I asked.

He kept going as if he hadn't heard me. No, that's not right. He heard me, I'm sure he did. But he kept on moving as if he didn't think I was talking to *him*.

Suddenly, he faced me. "Don't you have chores to do? Get going!"

He grumbled something else, too. I couldn't make out anything except that word again: "Angola." He snarled it, like he hated the sound of it. I didn't know what it meant outside of a country in Africa, and I couldn't believe Ronny knew any kind of geography. Plus, there was another word he said with it. It sounded like "fate," or "rate," or "hate." It was all nonsense to me — *Angola fate?* — but it obviously meant something to him.

The next afternoon, Samantha came over. I told her Ronny was still "finding his way." Uncle Carl had said that once, and I couldn't think of any other way to put it. She said she understood. Ronny was sitting in the courtyard, staring into space, when I walked her out to him.

"Oh my gosh, Ronny!" Sam said, sobbing and wrapping her arms around him. He didn't budge from his position in the chair. She pulled away, surprised, and glanced at me.

"I couldn't believe it when I heard," she said quietly.

Ronny's eyes were cold. "So?"

She ignored the word and pulled up a chair next to his. I went to my room. From my window over the patio, I could hear part of their conversation.

"Sam?" he was saying, sharply. "Why do you call yourself Sam? That's a man's name."

At first I thought it was a little routine they had. She giggled to begin with, then stopped. It wasn't a routine. But Ronny kept going. "People will confuse you for a man. It's not right. Besides, I already have a sweetheart."

"Oh? Who is that?" Sam asked, straightening in her chair.

Ronny looked ready to say a name, then frowned. "No one. Forget it."

It went on like that until he finally came out with a crazy, sobbing laugh. "Get away from me! Get out!"

She bolted up from her chair. "My gosh, who *are* you?"

I saw his shoulders move. A shrug, almost like

he didn't care. Samantha left in tears through the courtyard gate. Ronny sat silent in the wicker chair. I went down to him.

When I touched his shoulder, he jumped up, whirled on his heels, and lifted his hands as if to strike me.

"What are you doing?" I backed away.

"Get away from me," he growled. He stormed into the house. His door slammed a few moments later.

For the longest time I couldn't get Sam's sobs out of my mind. I found myself asking the same question she did.

Who are *you?*

But worse was coming.

That night, I was getting ready for bed and had fallen asleep waiting for Ronny to get out of the bathroom. I woke up gasping and sweating. It was after ten, nearly eleven. I'd just had the dream again about the dogs in the bayou. I couldn't breathe. I shook my head to clear it, then slid my feet to the floor.

The carpet was damp.

I saw that the hallway floor was wet, too.

"Ronny?" I called. No answer. I went into the hall. The bathroom light was on. I saw silvery water on the wooden floor outside and heard water rushing from the faucet.

"Ronny?"

I walked quickly down the hall to the bathroom. The water was on full-blast and the bathroom sink was overflowing. I shut it off.

"Ronny, what in the world —"

He was sitting on the edge of the bathtub, rocking back and forth, clutching his left index finger with his right hand.

"What happened to you?" I asked.

"I cut myself. Shaving. I sliced my finger. It's bad."

"With the electric razor?" I said, panicking. My voice went to a scared, squeaky pitch that I'm not proud of. "How do you slice yourself with an electric razor?"

Still rocking, Ronny looked up at me. "I didn't use the electric razor. I used . . . that." He nodded to the floor under the sink.

I looked. Lying in the water was a short paring knife.

My blood went cold. "You used a kitchen knife? Are you insane? You could have killed yourself with that —"

But something else was wrong.

There was no blood.

There was only water in the sink, on the floor. Not a drop of blood. Anywhere.

"You can't have cut it that bad," I said.

"I can see the bone."

My knees weakened. "Does it hurt?"

Ronny shook his head. "No. But shouldn't it? Shouldn't it hurt a lot? It seems deep."

"Let me see it," I said.

He looked into my eyes like a lost dog, then pulled his right hand away and held the sliced finger up to me.

I jerked back. His fingertip — the top half inch or so — was gashed nearly off. When he raised his hand, the tip swung away from the rest of the finger. I felt my stomach lurch, but there was no blood coming from the wound. Glancing inside the finger, I saw nothing but pale pink "stuff" — fiber and muscle and membrane — surrounding a glimpse of white bone.

"Oh, man," I said. I felt faint.

"Is it bad?" Ronny asked innocently. "Do you think it's bad?"

I turned away, plunged my hands into the sink water, and splashed my face. I needed to shock myself out of where my stomach wanted to go.

"Tape," I said. My voice sounded hoarse, a whisper. "We have first-aid tape in the cabinet. Let's use it."

"Okay. That sounds good. Tape," Ronny said like a helpless five-year-old with a boo-boo. I dug out a roll of tape and cut off a strip with the bathroom scissors. Together, Ronny and I set his fingertip back into place and wrapped the tape around it tightly.

He held up his bandaged finger and nodded. "This is good. Thanks, brother."

I nodded. "Tomorrow we should go to the doctor —"

"You *are* my brother, right?" Ronny interrupted. His eyes searched me for an answer. "You've said so before."

Then he stood up and splashed awkwardly out of the bathroom, turning in the doorway. "How far away am I?"

"How far away? From where?" This was too weird.

"From home. By train. How far?"

"But you're —"

"Doesn't matter," he snapped, disappearing down the hall.

Twenty-eight minutes later, after I had mopped up the mess and run the incident over in my mind, I heard Ronny leave his room, walk down the stairs, open the front door, and walk out. It was his first time out of the house since he quit his job.

I decided to follow him.

⊰ EIGHT ⊱

Club Noir

It was late now, almost midnight. The sky was black-ish purple, but the streets were still warm. In minutes, I was sweating under my arms, down my neck.

Why was I following him?

I didn't know. I didn't have any idea what I was doing. All I knew was that Ronny was scary, he was acting crazy, he was off . . . and he was all I had left. He had come back from the brink of death, who knows how, and he was having trouble. There was something wrong with him, but he was my brother. So I followed him.

Ronny walked a few blocks west, paused at a cor-ner, looked around and turned north, like he just then decided where he was going. I came to the same corner and saw him walking slowly up Toulouse Street. He stopped in front of a sliver of a storefront and puzzled at the sign above the door, moving his head one way and another as if trying to read

Russian. Finally, he stepped through the door into the darkness.

I moved closer. It was a music club, one of dozens on the street. I made my way there, careful not to be seen in case Ronny came right out again. He didn't.

The name of the place was Club Noir. A black doorway gaped. No light came from inside. There were no people crowded outside as there would have been if it were open, but I heard electric guitar strings being pinched and poked. The sound reminded me how much my father loved New Orleans blues. He had dozens of recordings from local clubs. But never mind.

I crept up to the door and listened. The guitar stopped, and there was low talking I couldn't make out, then quiet. The guitar started again. It was a song. A gruff old voice joined in.

The words he sang were garbled, but I recognized one of them.

Angola.

My nerves went electric.

A half hour later, I slunk into another storefront when Ronny came out of Club Noir, wiping his face and retracing his steps south. Was he crying? I watched him walk to the corner and turn onto our street. He was going back home.

I wasn't. I went inside.

The club was as humid as a rainstorm. Two electric fans whirred across the room, but they didn't move any cool air. Instead, they blew around the smell of warm rubber that I knew came from an overheated guitar amplifier.

Seated on a low stool next to the amp was a dark giant with grizzled hair. He must have been eighty, huddled over an electric guitar that, on him, looked no bigger than a ukulele.

He was wiping his face on the shoulder of his T-shirt. Had he and Ronny been crying together? What was going on? Just as I wondered whether to bolt out of there, he looked up.

"A little past your bedtime, isn't it?" he said in a low voice.

"My name is Derek Stone," I said.

Without responding, he went at the beat-up guitar in his lap, pinching its strings. They squealed under his fingers. Twisting the final note of his run back and forth — *eee-ooo-eee-ooo* — he held it, held it, then slid his fingers off the fret board. They fell into his lap.

"I'm Bob Lemon," he said. It was the lowest voice I had ever heard, and mellow, like the purr of a racing car. "Called Big Bob Lemon, mostly." His hand, when he extended it, was as large as a baseball mitt. I felt like a tiny ball of fresh mozzarella next to him.

"What can I do for you?" he went on. He looked at me with his head angled, and I realized that his right eye was false. I tried not to look at it.

I weighed what to say. "Look, sir, I don't know why I came, actually. I don't know. But I just saw my brother come in here. He's been having problems. . . ."

Big Bob Lemon shook his head slowly. He set his hands on the guitar again, then took them off without playing a note. He was silent for a very long minute.

"That boy is not your brother."

I laughed nervously. "You're kidding, right?"

He went back to playing. It was up to me to keep the conversation going.

"He's my brother. I followed him from our house."

"No, he's not," the man said, stopping again. "That boy may look like your brother. Talk like him, even. But it isn't him. It isn't him just like a ghost isn't a person."

I couldn't help it — I shivered. "A ghost? What are you talking about?"

"Think about it," Lemon went on. "Has he been acting like your brother? Like the brother you knew growing up?"

That stopped me. How did *he* know?

"He just came back from a terrible accident," I said.

"You sure it's your brother who came back?"

I felt my chest tighten as I got annoyed. "I don't know what you're talking about. You have no idea what he's been through."

"He was in the train that fell at Bordelon," he said.

I swallowed. "Right."

"So were you," he added. "Are *you* okay?"

"Me?"

"You were in the crash."

"So?"

"So you're you, but he's not him," Lemon said matter-of-factly, like it actually made sense. "And that's not his house you followed him from. Not anymore. He's somebody else now. I know him, but you don't."

I shook my head. "What are you talking about? *You* know him?"

"That is, I saw him before, only he didn't look like that."

My ear twinged sharply. "This is nuts —"

"Look, *he* came here," the man said. "He found me here because he knows me. He helped me once when I was a young boy, riding the rails. And he needed to talk about that."

I looked at Big Bob Lemon. "Ronny helped you when you were a young boy? Yeah. Right. I need to get out of here."

Lemon stood up. He towered over me, but his voice was still quiet and low. "What you need to do is follow him. You need to listen to him. Find out what you can. He may not be your brother anymore, but he's somebody. And he sure as day needs you."

None of that made any sense to me. Nothing made sense anymore.

"I heard you sing something about 'Angola,'" I said, changing the subject. "What does that mean?"

"Country in Africa, is all I know," Big Bob replied curtly. "Of course, you could look it up. You might find something different."

He sat down and started playing his guitar again. That was it. Conversation over.

◄ NINE ►

I Am Not Alone

I stepped onto the street and walked to the corner. It was very late now. The first neon signs were going off. From pink, blue, orange, red, the street was turning gray. *The trembling time*, I thought, though I couldn't tell you why I thought that or where those words came from.

I walked on. Stopped.

Are *you* okay?

Uh-huh. Yeah. You're a nut, old man, that's all —

Then I heard the deep voices again.

They came in waves, an incoming, outgoing tide of low anguished moaning, reaching toward me from the darkness, then pulling back. It must have looked weird to anyone who saw me tilting my head this way and that like a dog listening for its master's call. It would have looked weird, except there wasn't anyone to see me.

The street was empty.

When I turned the corner onto Royal Street, my

spine tingled up to my neck and into my bad ear. Whatever was making the sound had moved, too. Just not at the same pace I was moving. Sometimes it was closer, sometimes farther away. It was always the same tone, always echoing as if it came from some low place, a crypt or an underground chamber, out of the *damp-stone, stone-cold, cold-dead room*.

More words? Now I was really freaking myself out.

I hurried toward an arcade on the other side of the street and turned right, plowing into a group of tourists gawking at a menu outside an all-night café.

"Sorry," I said, hurrying on.

The voices got louder again. Was I crazy? I zigzagged across the next street and tore through the first open shop I saw, the twenty-four hour bookstore near my house, hoping for a clear path from front to back. No such luck. I had to weave between bookcases and spinning racks.

"Hey, kid," the cashier called. Her frown shot daggers. "Slow down!"

Several people spun around as I hustled to the back door. It was half open because someone had just come in. I barreled past her, spitting out an apology. "Sorry —"

"Jerk!" an older girl said.

Maybe the voices had been drowned out by the too-loud music in the store. Maybe it was the quiet of the back street. But the moment I stepped outside, the voices rushed at me again. They were following me.

But what *were* they? Dad's mother had heard songs before she died. Great, now I was acting like an eighty-year-old. Was it genetic? Had I really gotten messed up in the accident? My left ear was killing me. It felt like a long needle was slowly being pushed . . .

I ran to the end of the alley, froze, turned my head.

Could no one else hear the voices?

Are *you* okay?

I ran back into the bookstore.

"You again?" shouted the cashier. "See if I don't call the police on you —"

"Please don't," I said, heading for the front of the store again, when something went *snap* in my mind. The voices stopped. Just like that.

I froze next to a display table, holding it to steady myself. I listened. Nothing. No voices.

I looked around, my eyes finally focusing, and I saw books. Hundreds of books. History. Science. Technology.

Books.

They gave me an idea I should have had before.

"I'm dialing! Nine . . . one . . ." the cashier called out.

I couldn't say whether or not the voices were really gone. All I knew was that I needed to get home.

◄| TEN |►

The Oak Panel

My shirt was completely soaked by the time I slid into the house and locked the door behind me. I thought I'd locked it quietly, but Carl was on me in a second. He shuffled in quickly from the living room, angry with me for being out so late without calling. He had to drive first thing in the morning. Then he stopped, he just shut it off, and looked at me like Dad used to. Concerned.

"Is everything all right, Derek?"

Big Bob Lemon's voice echoed in my head. *Are* you *okay?* "Why?"

"Well, it's your face. Like you've seen . . . you're really pale."

"I'm okay," I said.

"Yeah?"

"Yeah. Sure."

Carl shooed me toward the stairs, but I said I needed a snack before bed and told him to go on up.

"Turn off the lights," he said, yawning as he climbed the stairs. "I'm glad you're all right." After his door clicked closed, I stood in the front hall, listening for a few minutes. Nothing. I took off my shoes and went upstairs.

The voices came back again, rumbling below everything, but they were outside now. Or somewhere else, anyway. I could still only hear them in my left ear. It sounded like the earbud of my iPod had fallen out of my right ear. Whatever. Maybe it was just the rumble of the city. Or maybe I was overly tired.

Ronny was asleep on his bed when I passed his room. His face was hard, frowning, even in sleep.

He looked confused. Or lost.

Ideas about what was going on swarmed in my mind, but none of them made sense.

How could Ronny actually be alive? I saw him fly out the train window. But how could he be dead for a month, and now suddenly not be? Why had he trapped and killed those rats? Why was he so mean to Sam? Why had he gone to Club Noir? How did he know Big Bob Lemon? What was "Angola"? *Look it up*, the man told me. *That boy is not your brother*, he told me. *Just like a ghost isn't a person*, he said.

And ghosts? No. No way. Never. That's fantasy. That's unreal. You hear a lot about ghosts in New

Orleans, with its long haunted history, cold houses, wispy apparitions. They were no more than dry floorboards and loose windows and fog.

I hated it, all of it. I had to know real information. Solid stuff. And now I knew where to start.

I crept quietly up to the third floor, to my father's office, and searched his desk. There were bills and maintenance reports, mortgage documents, receipts, estimates, scraps of paper scrawled with telephone messages or random numbers. Carl had arranged them in piles and was obviously dealing with them as best he could.

There was nothing there that could help me. I expected that. I knew where I would end up. But first, I booted up Dad's computer and did a search on the word "Angola."

Beyond the listings for the country in Africa, there were a few about Angola, Louisiana — where the main state prison was.

The state prison. I didn't know what to make of that.

Then I searched for Big Bob Lemon and came up with a brief encyclopedia entry on his career as a musician. It said that he was born in 1929 and lost an eye in an accident — a train accident — when he was nine.

Which would have been in 1938.

Huh.

I searched train accidents in 1938. All I found was a short list of book titles, most of them histories of railroading in Louisiana. I jotted down the titles. I had to move on.

I turned off the desk light and stood in the hall outside the office. From there, I could see a narrow set of plain oak stairs at the end of the hall. The lower steps were lit, while the upper ones lay in shadow, indistinct. I knew where the steps led. To the *faux chambre*. The fake room.

Only it wasn't fake, was it? It was Dad's private room, where he kept his trains and books. I had never been up there before. Not really because I respected Dad's privacy. No, it was more that I just didn't care. Old train models? Eh.

I headed up the stairs. There was no door at the top. Instead, I faced a wall of burnished oak panels. The central panel was narrow, but it went from ceiling to floor and was tall, almost like a pantry door. It was the most logical entrance to the room beyond, so I pushed.

Nothing.

I felt around the panel, trying to nudge it from side to side. It shifted slightly, though it seemed heavier than I expected and was more solidly built than I could have imagined. Following the edge of the panel with my fingers, I pushed, pulled, pressed all the way around. The seam between the panel and the frame made a slight cracking sound. Then I realized it didn't push in or pull out like a door at all. It dipped in and slid aside, disappearing into a space in the doorframe.

"A pocket door," I said softly.

When I moved the panel aside, a wave of stale air flowed over me. I crawled through the opening and stepped inside. The room was small, but not as small as it looked from the street.

A large desk and chair occupied the center of the room. Above and below the windows on the eight walls were bookcases; the uppermost shelf ran unbroken around the room and had a track on it that was filled with model trains. The ceiling of the octagonal room was made of eight panels sloping up to a point in the center, which I knew was directly under the gilt angel you could see from the street.

When I slid the door closed — *snap!* — the voices, distant as they were, were sheared off completely. It was quiet. I felt safe in a way I hadn't since the accident. I cracked a window, breathed in the night air over the city. Still no voices. Strange.

It was a handsome little room. And there were books. Hundreds of them. Louisiana history. Railroads. Locomotives. Engineering books. Geography books. Atlases. Labor history. It was running through the bookstore that had given me the idea to come up here in the first place. Dad had so many books that I'd had no interest in — until now.

With the list of book titles from the Internet in hand, I rummaged through Dad's shelves. His collection was arranged alphabetically by author, and I soon found two books on the list and three others that might help. I sat at his desk and first flipped to the indexes. My hands shook when I saw an entry for the term, "Angola Freight."

"What —?"

I turned to the page listed and found that "Angola Freight" was what they called the train that carried convicts to the penitentiary in Angola. The "freight" referred to was, of course, prisoners.

As I read further, my hands shook.

On the night of June 3, 1938, a bridge on the rail line between Alexandria and Angola collapsed. A train carrying prisoners crashed into Bordelon Gap.

"Are you kidding me?" I said aloud. I couldn't help talking to myself. What difference did it make? I'd already been acting completely nuts.

I scanned the next ten pages without seeing anything more about the crash. The next books had no other information about Angola Freight or the 1938 crash, either. Two of them did refer to the same article in a small newspaper called the *Marksville Ledger*, which seemed like it might have the most details of the crash.

I closed the last book, got up, and paced the room from window to window. I could see the floodlights around the cemetery and the glimmering water, the cemetery, the water, cemetery, water, as I tried to understand what I'd just read.

The desk lamp, dim as it was, shed an orangey-gold light in the room. The shelves holding Dad's collection of trains looked like they were burning.

I found myself peering at the center of the ceiling as I turned off the light. When I slid the door back in place, the voices, though faraway and disjointed, began again.

My sense of safety disappeared.

Books in hand, I went back down to Dad's office and searched the public library database on his computer. My heart leaped. Issues of the *Marksville Ledger* were in the main collection.

"Tomorrow," I muttered to myself. "Early."

Lying in bed a few minutes later, I stared at the ceiling. As I imagined the gold angel flying above me in the black sky, I realized that something had changed. I had something to do. And it was real.

Maybe it wouldn't make Ronny be himself again, and maybe it wouldn't bring Dad home, but it was the first real thing I'd be doing since the accident.

At the very least, I was going to find out *something*.

But I had no idea what.

⊰ ELEVEN ⊱

Fears

When nine o'clock rolled around the next morning, I headed to the main library, a streetcar ride and a short walk away on Loyola Street.

It was a gray day, not too hot, but I was already sweating. I wasn't fully awake, either. Still, it felt good to be going to gather information, comforting, like a defense, like building a kind of armor. It would be a long road, and I was just beginning, but I was heading in the right direction.

I could just tell.

A young guy sat behind the library's periodicals desk with a fan blowing in his face. He had a beard that looked like dirt, but he smiled when I walked in. I showed him my library card.

"Whoa, you're the guy whose brother died and then didn't, huh?" he asked.

"That's me," I said, unfazed. I told him what I wanted. He tapped away on his keyboard, shook his head, frowned, then looked up.

"The *Marksville Ledger* isn't digital," he said.

"Okay . . ."

"And the microfilm is stored up in the State House. But we have the original newspapers."

"Can I see them?" I asked.

"Not here," he said. "They're in the annex on Marais Street. Behind Armstrong Park."

I calculated the distance in my head. "Can I go there? I mean, is it open? Will they let me in?"

"Yes, yes, and yes," the guy said, pleased with himself for being able to answer that way. "I'll call and tell them you're coming. Not many people go there, so they have to open the collection especially for you. But that's what they get paid for, so, you know . . ."

"Thanks a lot," I said.

It was near ten now, and the morning was still gray, though hotter. I sweated more, walking through the open park to the buildings beyond.

Library annex? I thought for sure the guy was sending me to a trailer with lightbulbs hanging from the ceiling. He wasn't. The annex was a big old marble building, a former bank in the heart of a neighborhood that time had passed by.

I pulled the door open. An older woman sat behind a metal desk, looking drowsy. She jerked up when the door squeaked.

I looked past her, deep into a palace of dust. There must have been hundreds of stacks of moldy records, handwritten documents, deeds, crumbling books, thick old ledgers, brown newspapers, personal archives, one-of-a-kind publications, paper, paper, paper. It was like a scene out of Dickens.

The lady rang a bell, and something in the dark end of a hallway to my right began to creak toward me. I wanted to run, but the lady showed no signs of fear, so I tried not to, either. What seemed like hours later, an untucked old attendant with a jowly, unshaven face emerged, limping across the floorboards to the desk. He smelled like charred coffee and mothballs.

I half-expected him to speak in some unintelligible language, but he didn't say a word. He only turned away and ushered me wordlessly down another corridor and a steep set of stairs, to an underground series of rooms. Stack after stack, shelf after shelf, I felt like I was moving backward through time.

I didn't like the feeling.

The old guy slumped in a chair, huffing out a great musty breath. Still saying nothing, he pointed across the room to the shelves and shelves of newspapers. I started in on them. After a while, I dug up issues of the *Marksville Ledger*. I found the article about the accident on the first page of a paper dated June 5, 1938, two days after the first train tumbled into Bordelon Gap.

I wiped a layer of dust off the reading table, sat, and began to read. The details of the crash were eerily similar to mine. Most of the convict train's cars made it across the bridge, when stress on the rails caused the bridge to buckle. The end car went sliding into the ravine, resulting in seventeen fatalities.

"Trestles snapped . . . car fell backward . . . struck the ravine's deep slope . . . buckled . . . fire . . ."

The very same.

There was a grainy photo of the river twisting below the crash site, looking the same as when I had been there. My eyes closed and I saw it again, churning like a black snake. *River of many deaths.*

I read that not everyone killed in the 1938 crash was a criminal. There was a woman, the wife of a convict who was accompanying her husband, an arsonist, to jail. They let her on the train because he was going to be executed. She was ill and probably wouldn't live to see her husband again. Two guards also died in the crash. One was trapped in the wreck and killed in the fire. The other man, a young guard on his first day at work, was thrown from the car as it broke in half.

Broke in half? What a first day.

That's when I read something that freaked me out entirely. The young guard was a guy named Virgil Black who came from a little town called Shongaloo, but the name of the older guard was Jubal Higgins.

Jubal Higgins!

Ronny had said that. He'd said, *Daddy Jubal*. What did it mean?

There was more.

Among the survivors was "a Negro boy aged nine, Robert Lemon, who suffered head injuries and possible blindness."

"What!" I slapped the paper down on the table and stood up. "Big Bob Lemon, who was nine years old in 1938? Is this seriously saying that Big Bob Lemon is the boy from the crash? How did Ronny know?"

"Shhh," said the attendant, who had woken up.

Fine. Fine. But how could Ronny possibly know about *any* of this? Angola Freight? Daddy Jubal? As Tooley had said, Ronny was the last person to read history books or use a computer to find information. Where did he get these facts? And why was he talking to strangers about this?

Or *was* he a stranger to Big Bob Lemon?

Lemon had said that Ronny was someone else. He'd said he *knew* Ronny. That he helped him when he was a young boy riding the rails.

What! What! What!

I didn't believe — I *couldn't* believe — where my mind was taking me. But what exactly were the facts?

Two trains crashed in the same place.

Ronny survived but was acting weird, saying and doing things that weren't like him.

He talked about the Angola Freight.

He talked to a victim of the first crash.

I read and reread the article a dozen times, then finally photocopied it, left, and walked back through the park to the main library. I collected a bunch of geography and travel books, and found a secluded table near the stairs on the top floor. It felt better to be up high, and I was near the stairs in case I heard more weird voices.

Thumbing through the books, I read about how Bordelon Gap was a ravine between two halves of a low mountain. The river running through the Gap was part of the Red River, which ran across the entire state from northwest to southeast. It was nearly inaccessible from the Gap, and treacherous because of its rapids and the speed of its current.

I read as much as I could, until there was no more to read. Not in that section of the library, at least. Unable to stop myself, I edged into the stacks on

Louisiana legends. Ghost stories. I couldn't believe I was doing this.

I scanned shelves of books on the paranormal. Stories about hauntings. Doctored photographs. I flipped through them, my stomach turning with each page. It was all so . . . made up! I hated that kind of book. Bogus history. Wishful thinking. Hocus-pocus! And yet, before slamming the books shut I checked every table of contents, endnote, and index. I wrote down what I read about auditory manifestations, apparitions, hauntings, spiritual places.

When I stopped for a minute, I realized that I was breathing heavily. I thought about all the things Ronny had done since he came back. One after another, they piled up and scared the life out of me. It terrified me to think of it: Ronny didn't know me, he wasn't himself, he wasn't the brother I'd had for fourteen years. He was . . . *someone else*.

Finally, it was a book called *Afterlives* by a man named Tomas Deak that stopped me cold. It said the usual weirdness about why things like ghosts actually exist. I was about to toss it aside with the others when I came upon what the author said could happen at the exact moment of death.

The movement of souls — from one body to another.

◀ TWELVE ▶

Gobbledygook?

Lunchtime came and went while I read the book from cover to cover.

The movement of souls.

It sounded horrific and impossible and insane and wrong.

But I forced myself to read it. Through page after page, my shoulders and neck felt besieged by tiny spiders. My legs turned to ice. I breathed the shallowest breaths.

The book basically argued that when a body dies, its soul moves off, leaving the dead form and going to some kind of afterlife. Most people believe something like that happens, and then it's over.

Except maybe it's not over.

Not always.

For the tiniest fraction of the brief moment of death — like the time between, say, Tuesday and Wednesday — the place the soul vacates is left open like a kind of vacuum. In that moment, a second soul — one that's been waiting — can enter and reanimate that dead body. The body "lives" again with a different soul.

Do you understand what I'm telling you here? Some people actually believe that at the instant of death, a long-dead soul can trade places with a dying soul.

And the dead soul lives again.

Not as a ghost, no. Something worse.

I thought of zombies, the walking dead, but that wasn't right, either. Another soul was in the body now.

It made me think of a kind of translation from one body to another.

Translation.

Impossible?

Absolutely . . . right?

The author, who was an anatomist, took it even further. He theorized that two souls could probably only exchange places if their causes of death were identical. The two bodies had to arrive at the moment of death the very same way, or it wouldn't work. That's why it was so rare.

Rare. But not impossible. The accident Ronny, Dad, and I were in was nearly identical to the 1938 accident at the same place.

I didn't want to keep reading, but I couldn't stop myself.

The author went on to say that some people believe the worlds of the living and the dead exist side by side, separated only by a kind of fabric. There are texts going back thousands of years about this division of worlds. Spirits are immaterial, they have no solid form, so they can slip back and forth between the worlds. They can haunt us if they want to.

Fine. That's ghosts.

But what if sometime, somehow, the fabric is torn? What if it actually gets a rip in it? Why and how this might happen nobody knows, but if it did, a dead soul — the part of a person that never really dies — might escape from the afterlife through the tear and translate into a dying body.

Making it live again.

Making it live again?

I wanted to stomp on that book and throw it out the window. I wanted to scream and run out of that stupid library and never come back. But I didn't move.

I remembered the nauseous sense of free fall on the train. My father's coiling scream. Ronny's flight through the window. The jagged ravine. I knew that if I let myself, I would imagine the wreck over and over and not be able to stop.

I stood up. If I believed the book, I'd have to believe that dead souls were waiting in the Bordelon Gap, waiting for a second train to crash right where theirs did. I tried to imagine a tear in the fabric separating life and death. I tried to imagine the souls of the dead crowded at the opening like captives at a door to freedom. When the train fell and people died, the circumstances were exactly the same as the crash in 1938. Dead souls escaped the afterlife and translated into the dying bodies.

So the book was asking me to believe that inside Ronny was someone who died in the first train wreck, that my brother was dead, but that his body was now inhabited by someone else? But who?

I searched the photocopy of the newspaper. Virgil Black. The young guard.

The idea of a long-dead soul entering a just-dead body made me sick with horror. It sounded repulsive and painful. I tried to swallow, tried to breathe, when all of a sudden — *bang!* — the stair door flew open and Ronny charged at me.

"You!" he cried.

I fell back into my chair. "How — how did you know to look for me here?"

His expression was like a madman's. Was he in pain? His hair was wild, his eyes bloodshot. He stormed up and down the stacks, his head turning madly from side to side.

A security guard edged through the stacks toward us. He was reaching for his walkie-talkie.

"We're fine, sir," I said. "Ronny, outside. Outside."

We hurried down the stairs to the square outside the library. It was hot, the sun burning behind the haze. A crowd had gathered to listen to a couple playing a violin and a banjo badly. I pulled Ronny into the shadows of a nearby arcade.

"What's wrong?" I asked.

"What's happening to me?" he groaned. "I feel like I'm being taken over. I don't know what's going on in my head —"

"Ronny, cool down," I said. My heart thundered.

"This is insanity. That's what this is. I'm going crazy. I don't know who I am anymore. I never should have left Shongaloo. That's when it all went wrong —"

"Have left *where*?" I said.

Without warning, he bolted down the arcade toward the street.

I tore the photocopied article out of my pocket. My eyes could hardly focus, but I strained to read it, and there was the word — Shongaloo. It was the young prison guard's hometown. I read his name again. Then I heard deep voices. Moaning.

Ronny stopped running and walked back to me, his eyes pleading. "You hear them, too?"

"I . . . think I do," I said. "Don't ask me how . . ."

He slapped his hands on my shoulders, his eyes welling with tears. "You don't know what this means! You hear them, too! The voices are getting closer all the time. They've come back —"

I shivered. "Who? Who are they? Ronny, look. We should go home. There's something I need to show you —"

His face turned dark. "This isn't my home. I — I have to get out. I have to go —"

He tried to twist out of my grip.

"Don't leave," I said, holding on to his cold wrist.

"I had to leave you!" he snarled. "I had to get a job to help Momma. I had to — let go of me!" He jerked his arm away and stomped down the arcade toward the street.

"Wait," I said. "Wait . . . Virgil . . ."

⊸ THIRTEEN ⊷

The Past Is Not Past

Ronny froze in his tracks. He was still Ronny to me, even if he . . . wasn't. He turned slowly back to face me. "What did you call me?"

"Vir — Virgil," I said softly, stumbling over the name I dreaded saying. "Virgil Black . . ."

Color flushed his cheeks. "You know me?"

So it was true.

I pulled him to a bench under the arcade.

"How can you know me . . . ?" he asked.

"Look," I said as calmly as I could, trying to settle myself as much as him. "Maybe I do. Maybe I don't. Never mind that now. You need to tell me what you remember. About before."

Ronny's eyes darted around. "What? Before?"

I couldn't believe my own words. "Before the train wreck. What do you remember?"

He made a sound in his throat like gagging, then rolled his palms into his temples. His face twisted in pain. He clenched his eyes shut. When he opened them, they stared blankly into the distance.

"It was my first job after leaving home," he said. "My first day. I had been hired as a guard. I came from Shongaloo. I caught vermin, rats, mice in the barns. Just like I taught you . . . or someone, maybe not you. This was my first real job. Momma cried the day I left."

It was hard to believe I was hearing this. It proved just how close those thoughts were to him, wherever they came from.

"Go on."

"We were putting them on the train, helping them up the steps."

"Helping who?" I asked.

"It's hard to get up the steps with the ankle brace-lets they wore."

"Who did? What steps?"

"The convicts, up the steps into the train car. Me and Daddy Jubal helped them. He was head guard that day."

It was like listening to an old man remember his long-ago youth, except I was looking at a nineteen-year-old boy. It was Ronny, only it wasn't. It wasn't even his voice anymore. It was lower, thicker.

"Of course, I was mighty scared," he went on.

"Why?"

"Because of Erskine Cane. He was the main one we were transporting that day. He was out of his mind. A killer. He had this crazy smile on his face. It had been there since I first saw him, and it wouldn't leave. Didn't matter that he was going to Angola to die. Didn't mean a thing to him. He was a big man, and strong. Convicted of burning houses for fun. Three families died before he was caught. He was going to prison to be executed."

I remembered the newspapers in the library annex. "There was a woman, too, right?"

Ronny nodded. "His wife. As loony as he was. No smile, though. A face like a corpse. She was crazy and dying, and looked more than halfway there —"

He froze. A streetcar traveled slowly past the square where we sat. Ronny shivered and looked away.

"And the accident?" I asked quietly. I didn't want to hear it, but I had to.

He described it just as the old newspaper had. It sounded almost exactly the same as the collapse we — Ronny and I — had gone through together.

"I was thrown from the window of the train car. I saw it explode. I fell hard. There was a boy I tried to help . . . he was bleeding, I moved him . . ."

"He was nine," I whispered. "Bob Lemon."

He rocked back and forth on the bench, nodding. "Then I lost my footing and fell into the chasm . . . onto the rocks . . . the rocks was where . . ." He stopped.

I couldn't imagine it, the horror of it. "And after that?"

He searched my face. "*After* that?"

"When you were . . . in the ravine."

Ronny shut his eyes again and rubbed his temples. "I can't . . . see it."

The voices rang in my head suddenly. I bolted up. He did, too.

"You hear them again?" he asked.

"I shouldn't be able to, right?" I said, pressing my ear closed. "I survived the accident."

"I don't know," he said.

The voices rolled and twisted over one another.

"Who are they?" I asked, wincing.

"I don't know," Ronny said again. "The dead?"

I snorted a laugh. "Boy, we're a couple of people who don't know a lot, aren't we?"

I thought I saw a hint of a smile. "I don't know. I don't know anything."

I looked into his eyes then and felt as if we had broken through a wall and were together again, Ronny and me. Only it wasn't Ronny anymore.

It was someone named Virgil.

"We have to go back to the bridge," I said. "You have to see it, to remember what happened there. And we need to find out what we can about our . . . my . . . dad."

"You mean, maybe he's alive?"

"He could still be there, hurt," I said.

He searched my eyes. "Bordelon Gap?"

"Bordelon Gap."

He nodded slowly. "I'll drive."

⊰ FOURTEEN ⊱

Dark River

So, was that it?

I didn't fight it anymore? Had I accepted that Ronny was . . . gone? And did I really believe that in his place was someone else, someone who died seventy years ago, someone named Virgil Black?

I don't know what to tell you.

I don't know what to tell you, except that I had driven with Ronny lots of times, and no way was my brother behind the wheel on the way to Bordelon Gap. It was amazing that Virgil Black hadn't died in a car crash long before he ever got on that convict train. For him, a steering wheel was a deadly weapon.

Those crazy cop chases on TV had nothing on this guy.

"Hoo-wee!" he yelled like the farm boy he used to be. "I started driving when I was thirteen, but this . . . *this*!"

He didn't seem to care about speed limits or stop

signs. He drove into every pothole as if he was aiming at it. He cut people off. He never used his turn signal. He drove completely off the road and careened back onto sidewalks, over lawns, between light poles.

When we reached Bordelon Gap, I stumbled out of the car, feeling like I'd just survived a five-hour roller-coaster ride with a madman.

"Never drove on real roads much, did you?" I asked him.

Ronny grinned. "Nope. But I will now!"

It was good — really good — to joke with him, like old times. But as soon as he caught sight of the chasm and the river below, his flash of humor was gone.

I was alone with a dead man again.

"Let's get closer," he said.

Giant trucks blocked the rails on both sides of the fallen bridge. The whole area was crawling with police and construction crews. The rescue work was done; now they were rebuilding the bridge. Men in yellow hard hats were scouring the site, picking up debris.

The ravine was steep all the way to the bottom. My legs turned to jelly when I peered down at the black water, and I thought of those words again.

Dark river, rolling river, river of many deaths. I couldn't imagine anyone coming up out of that.

And then the terror of water fell over me. That was it, wasn't it? I saw water and my own nightmare returned.

I was looking down Bordelon Gap, but all I could see was the place I'd tried so hard to forget.

Bayou Malpierre.

I was young, barely four years old. For some reason I've tried hard to remember but can't, I was walking in a bayou thick with trees that arched over black water. It was nearly night and hot and raining. Who was I with? I don't know. Darkness fell quickly. I got separated.

There I was, a little boy lost among the dark trees, the moss and the stink of vegetation and the slow black water and the rain. I remember calling out, but softly. I didn't want to wake the ghosts I thought lived in the water.

And the rain came down harder.

I whispered for help. How dumb was that? I whispered for help, so of course, no one heard me. With every moment, I was becoming more lost, trying to find my way through the dense trees.

Then there were the dogs. Five, six, seven, barking and squealing and wailing in the close, soggy growth around me. Not search dogs. Wild dogs, bayou dogs. They smelled my fear. They were gathering and howling and coming closer. I heard their paws sloshing in the water. Eerie keening, echoing in the swampy darkness.

Gasping for air, stone-cold frightened, I ran over the soft ground. Reeds whipped my face.

Then there were stones. Headstones. Where was I? A cemetery? In the bayou?

I slipped on the spongy ground, struck the back of my head on a stone, slid into the black water. I tried to pull myself up, but the rain pounded me down. The swamp was deep. Hands and old dead faces gathered around me in the rank water, drawing me to them.

And the dogs came closer, closer. Water covered my face, went into my mouth, my nose. I tried to scream. I swallowed mouthfuls of the foul black liquid.

Suddenly, there was a popping sound. Gunshots. Dogs wailed and howled and something — a hand — reached through the water for me. Warm and strong. I was heaved back up onto land. Pressure on my chest, lungs bursting, someone else's air in my mouth and throat.

I screamed water.

I remember my whole body heaving, swallowing air. Then I was alone.

I was four years old. Alone in a bayou. Why was I there? Who had saved me? Who had run the dogs off, pulled me out of the dark swamp, given me his breath?

No one would talk about it. Dad said no, it wasn't him, that maybe I dreamed the whole thing. Why would a four-year-old be alone in the bayou?

I asked Mom once. We were on a narrow street, buildings all around. She touched my damaged ear, claimed maybe I saw a movie — she named two or three I could have glimpsed some scenes of and might be remembering. She left for France soon after. Ronny said that if it did happen like I said, it must have been when he was away at a swim meet. But he was nine when it happened. He wasn't swimming in meets yet.

No one believed me.

Bzzzz! I was near the crest of the chasm, looking down, shivering, when my pocket hummed. *Bzzzz!*

A policeman turned at the sound. Ronny pulled me down behind a rock. "What's that?"

"Cell phone," I whispered. "Sorry —"

"Make it shut up!" he hissed.

I plunged my hand into my pocket and switched the phone off. We couldn't be spotted. We weren't supposed to be there. I looked up.

The officer scanned the hill. He turned back to

talk to a man in a gray jumpsuit, who removed his hard hat and mopped his forehead with a gloved hand.

Ronny was frowning something fierce. His eyes were fixed on the twisting river at the bottom of the ravine.

I tugged on his sleeve. "Come on, Ronny. We need to back away."

He didn't move.

I hated to do it, but I said his other name again. "Virgil . . ."

He stared down at the water, his forehead furrowing.

"Darkness," he said finally. "For a long time, there was only darkness. It felt like I was floating, swimming in nothing. For years. For a long time."

"You remember that?" I said, feeling cold all of a sudden.

Ronny sucked in a huge breath, said nothing.

"Then what?" I asked.

"Others," he said. "Others were with me. I can feel them even now, hear them whisper, sense them doing that thing they do instead of breathing. It's like moaning. Voices without bodies."

"Who are they?" I asked.

"Daddy Jubal. The others. The mad wife. They're . . . angry. Fighting."

His face went icy white. His eyelids flickered. "We were crowded at the door. Only it wasn't a door. It was like . . . a gash, ripped across the air. There was a tear of light, sudden, from top to bottom. And water. We all started to rise to it."

What Ronny was talking about wasn't the great white light you see near death. This was something else. Torn fabric, the opening between the worlds. The souls of the dead were crowded at it — waiting to cross over.

Ronny rubbed his eyes. "In the light, I saw a train swimming down through the air. Like the accident that killed me, only it wasn't me this time. It was someone else falling. Something pushed me toward the opening. I could see the falling boy, hear his cries as he fell onto the rocks. I swept up out of the water and went to him. Then I . . . I . . . I was that boy, falling into the river, going under until I stopped. There was a crook in the river, a bank that arched out, holding me safe like an arm. Hours passed, days passed. I am the boy now."

The full realization of what I had read now stabbed its way into my head. He was talking about dead souls. He was talking about translation.

"It was Ronny," I said.

He turned. "You call me that."

I wanted to cry.

"The others came with me through the opening," he went on. "*He* was there. The big, dark shape, like an ox. I'm afraid of him."

A siren whirred on the slope above us. I pulled Ronny's head lower.

"Do they see us?" he asked.

"Not yet," I said. "Who are you afraid of?"

"Cane," he whispered. "Erskine Cane, the arsonist. The killer. He came back, too. He . . . wants something here."

Ronny paused, still staring at the water below. "They're here. I feel their pain, the pain of being here again. I hear their voices. You do, too."

But why, I wondered. Why?

"They know I'm here," he said. "They know I know about them."

Did they know about me, too? How could they?

I survived the accident.

I never died.

I wanted to say it was insane, but I couldn't form the words, not even in my head. He was talking about the torn fabric and about translation. Virgil Black, long-dead victim of the first bridge collapse, was telling me how he looked out from the world of the dead, saw Ronny die the same way he had, and took his place.

So that's it, then.

Translation happens.

"You there!" yelled a voice. I looked up. The police officer was edging quickly down the hillside.

"What are you two doing?" he shouted. Sirens wailed.

"Dang," said Ronny, watching a black-and-white cruiser roar up over the crest. Another. A third.

He ran along the ledge, then stopped in his tracks. His face twisted. He slapped a hand over one ear.

"What's the matter?" I asked. "Come on —"

"Quiet!" he snapped. His body tensed as if he was ready to fight. "Oh, no . . ." He turned and scanned the ravine.

I saw them at the same time he did, a little below us. Two men.

One was short and wiry, like a greyhound in a dark uniform. He stood on the crest of the ravine below us. His head moved jerkily like a squirrel, while his torso remained motionless.

"Who is he? What's he doing?" I whispered.

Ronny stared. "Getting used to his new body, to being here again. I don't know him, but the big one has to be Cane. It's Erskine Cane."

The big man was as large as a house, and his head was nearly shaved. He was fairly busting out of his shirt. It hung nearly in shreds on his shoulders and arms, but I could tell that it was a camouflage shirt.

My heart shuddered. He was one of the soldiers who had given Abby Donner and her mother their seats on the train. Only now he looked terrifying. Mad. Crazy.

His face was angular and twisted into a bizarre smile. Even at that distance it scared me to my bones.

"I remember them both," I said. "They were soldiers on the train."

A siren stopped directly above us, and Ronny took my arm. His grip was cold, strong. He hustled me along the edge of the ravine, away from the stumbling policeman. Soon we were racing along a ledge in the hillside until the earth flattened out into a sort of meadow, its black grass scorched from the train fire.

"Come on," Ronny growled. "Come on."

So the farm boy who became a guard, died, and came back, pulled me along through the grass.

"Hurry," he said.

Scared, confused, angry, I followed.

◄| FIFTEEN |►

Them

When we found a place that was out of sight, we poked our heads up and saw the two men scouring the bushes near the ledge.

What were they looking for?

I didn't want to think about it.

Cane gestured to the smaller man, and they moved up from the crest. The police still couldn't see them.

"I need to follow them," said Ronny.

"What? Follow them? We can't —"

"Who said 'we'?"

"You're not leaving me here!" I said.

But he was already scrambling away between brush and rock, heading deeper into the ravine. The police were hurrying down toward us. "Wait up!" I whispered.

Ronny — or Virgil, whatever — was amazingly sure-footed. After a few moments I couldn't see him anymore. I hurried to catch up but tripped over a rock, fell, and rolled twice, finally grasping at some roots to keep me from falling farther downhill.

The voices changed. They became garbled. My ear hurt, and I suddenly felt sick. Then I saw the wiry soldier creeping up behind Ronny. They knew we were there.

"Ronny!" I yelled. He didn't hear me. I tried the other name. "Virgil! Behind you!" It was too late. The smaller man grabbed Ronny from behind and held him still. Erskine Cane rose out of the bushes.

Cane towered over Ronny. His hands quivered at his sides, fingers flexing open, closed. He growled something, and Ronny spat something back at him. I was too far away to hear what they said. Were they arguing? I could make out a word, two. Then Ronny groaned as Cane pulled back and batted his face, while the other man held Ronny's arms tight behind his back.

I couldn't just stand there. "Stop it!" I yelled.

The savage head of Erskine Cane swiveled toward me. I went cold. Police cars were screeching to a stop on the ledge above. The officers on foot were still far behind us. Doors opened, slammed shut.

Cane had a military knife hanging on his belt, but he turned back to Ronny and relied on his giant fists, instead. Ronny's head was whipped back and forth by blow after blow, but he didn't make a sound.

Could he feel pain?

"Stop it!" I shouted again.

Cane was growling angrily with each breath. I crawled forward, then heard a rush of undergrowth crackling and crashing above me. Three officers hurried down the slope toward us, pistols out.

"Down on your knees, hands behind your heads!" one yelled.

Ronny fell limp to the ground as Cane and his sidekick bolted into the tall grass. Before they were out of view, Cane turned. His eyes flashed at me. I froze until the other man pulled him away.

One officer stumbled on the steep slope above, his pistol firing wildly. The others stopped. The cop was all right but, distracted, they were done chasing us for now. I pulled Ronny behind me, edging up the incline. He looked hurt, but there was no blood on his face. We raced toward the car, dived in. Ronny floored it again. This time, I was glad he drove with a lead foot.

He hunched over the wheel, silent, somber, eyes fixed on the highway ahead.

"What did he say to you?" I asked. "Cane. What did he say?"

No answer.

Maybe he knew I had heard his response to Cane. *You won't take him.*

"I heard something," I said. "Is he . . . are they after me? Are they after *me*?"

"I don't know," Ronny said softly. "Forget it for now. We need fuel. You have money?"

"Look —" I started.

"Forget it!" he said. "We need fuel!"

We drove into a small town, somewhere near Plauchville or Dupont. The town was nothing much — gas station, coffee shop, food mart, a handful of wooden houses, a trailer park. Three times as many cars were on blocks in the yards as on the street.

While Ronny gassed up the car, I went into the coffee shop.

It was the least dead thing I saw, and even it was empty except for one woman with her back to me, alone in a booth. Her hair was brown, stringy. She wore an ill-fitting denim jacket, a man's. She didn't look up when I entered, just went on drinking her coffee. She jerked it up to her mouth with both hands and bent to the cup halfway, as if she wanted to dive into it herself.

I didn't know why I looked at her for so long.

"Can I help you?" asked a smiling guy behind the counter. He couldn't have been much older than Ronny. Ronny could have had a simple job like that, taking orders, running the soda machine. Ronny could have done so much more than that. But not now. It made me sick.

I ordered a grilled cheese and a soda. The boy gave me a quick nod, swiveled to the soda machine, passed me my Coke, and disappeared into the kitchen.

I heard a spatula clank. The grill hissed.

I pulled out my cell phone. There were two missed calls and one voice mail from the same number — the New Orleans coroner. I listened to the message.

"Hello? Hello? Dang. This is John Runyon at the coroner's office? We have some information about . . . Carson Stone? From the accident?" Everything he said sounded like a question. "We got some bad news? Somebody call us back?"

He left the number and hung up.

The door squeaked. Ronny? I glanced up. No. A man came in and sat across from the stringy-haired woman, head low.

Next, the woman rose and crossed behind my back toward the restrooms. I thought for a minute that the boy in the kitchen had turned on the radio.

It wasn't the radio.

As the woman moved behind me, there was humming in my left ear. My cheeks flushed. My forehead got warm. It built and built as she approached, and died off as soon as she went by. It was a dull, low whisper by the time the ladies' room door closed behind her. I didn't get a good look at her. But I had heard words this time.

"...*first*...*first*..."

I shivered, colder than cold.

What did it mean? Was she one of them? Was she the crazy woman — Erskine Cane's wife?

Then it struck me who the woman — the body — might be. I almost fell off my stool. Abby Donner's mother? Had she died like the others and was now ... translated?

It felt as if a needle were slowly being inserted into my neck behind my earlobe. I saw water, black water, as dark as the coffee in the counter pot. The woman emerged from the restroom. I turned to look at her, but her head was bent low. Her hair hung down, hiding her cheeks. She didn't look up, just walked slowly, mechanically, back to her seat.

The hum became a roar in my ears. "...*first*..." My blood went cold.

I paid, left, and hurried to the gas station. Ronny was sitting in the car.

"Anything?" he asked.

He said nothing when I told him what I had seen. I couldn't bring myself to understand what it meant if the woman I saw was actually the poor girl's mother. I was numb.

Three hours later, we were back in New Orleans. Ronny drove into the parking lot of the City Hall complex. I listened one last time to the coroner's voice mail.

"We got some bad news."

When we walked into the building, I wondered if I would know anymore what bad news really was.

◀| SIXTEEN |▶

The Dead Room

I was a wreck by the time we got down to the coroner's office, a gloomy set of rooms in the basement of the building behind City Hall. It was cold and smelled of chemicals.

Ronny, grim-faced, sullen, shuffled along behind me as if I were pulling him along.

The outer office was all oak chairs and benches. A secretary sat behind a wide desk. Beyond her, there were glass doors and streaky windows with the shades half pulled down.

"You here to see him?" she asked, without raising her head.

"Yes," I said. "It's about our father. Carson Stone."

"I know," she said, still not raising her head.

Saying his name, I saw Dad slide from the broken train. His cry was long, as if he were alive at least until the ridge at the top of the chasm.

Maybe the wreck didn't kill him.

Maybe he did survive.

Or was that blind hope? It had already been nearly a month.

The secretary pressed a button on her desk. A loud buzzer sounded, and a wooden door with reinforced glass clicked open on the other side of the little room.

"Go on in," she said.

Ronny followed a few steps after me, silent as a stone.

Inside was a room of shadows. Chilled and windowless, it had floor lamps at low wattage and one wall lined with refrigerated steel cabinets. I'd seen morgues on TV. I knew there were corpses in the drawers.

To one side, a huge man with spectacles at the end of his nose was leaning over a steel table, peering closely at something under an intense light.

Ronny stepped backward into the shadows.

"What are you doing?" I whispered.

"How much do I owe ya?" the man said then, without looking up from his table.

His white coat was open to show a wild printed shirt and cargo shorts. The armpits of the coat were dampened with sweat. I could see the floral pattern of his shirt right through them.

"Excuse me?" I said.

"Did you bring the po'boy?" the man asked, finally

glancing up at my empty hands. "I called back and asked for a roast pork with double cheese? Did you bring that, too?"

The look in my eyes must have told him.

"Wait. Pizza boy?"

I shook my head. "No. Someone called about our father."

Behind me, Ronny shifted his feet.

The man's face cleared. "You're *not* the pizza boy," he grunted. "So never mind." He toddled away from the steel table to a desk and rustled through a stack of papers. He slid one out.

"Your father is Carson Stone?" he asked.

"Yes, sir."

"Your mother around?"

"No. She's in France and isn't coming back."

"Then I got some news for you," he said, placing the paper back on the stack.

At that moment, the buzzer went off. The door clicked open again, and a girl walked in.

"Pizza," she said.

The coroner frowned at her, then laughed. "So *you're* the pizza boy!"

She didn't laugh. "Nineteen dollars, seventy-eight cents," she said.

"You bring the po'boy?" he asked.

"Porker, double cheese," she droned, sizing up his

barrel-waist. "And so good for you, too. That's nine-teen dollars, seventy-eight cents."

He pulled out two tens and told her to keep the change.

"Gosh, what will I do with it all?" the pizza girl grumbled, slamming the door behind her.

In a single move, the man tore open the pizza box, detached a slice, and folded it deftly into his mouth.

"Your father's hand," he said, nodding me over to the table and prying open what looked like a plastic food container with his free fingers. Inside lay an assortment of pink things.

Blood rushed up my neck to my jaw, and my ear began to sting again. Did I hear voices? I turned, glanced at Ronny. He was immobile in the darkness, leaning against a file cabinet, eyes pinched shut.

"This here's a knuckle," the coroner said. With the bitten end of his pizza, he pointed to a knot of some-thing at the bottom of the container. "I'm pretty sure of that. This other thing is part of a wrist. That little guy there might or might not be a finger. . . ." He went back to the steel table. "The DNA of these pieces says it's Carson Stone."

Hearing my father's name as I looked into the mess of stuff, my throat thickened up. "So what does this mean?" I croaked.

"Since they found these bits on the edge of the ravine," the coroner said, forcing the remainder of the slice into his mouth, "I'm pretty certain it means your father's dead. From there it's a sheer drop of near a hundred feet into a fast-moving river. If this is the only part of him they found, and they found it *there*, then you gotta conclude that the rest of him fell down the Gap into the river. It's like this, son. If the train wreck didn't kill him, if the rocks didn't kill him, if the long fall into the river didn't kill him, he surely would have drowned. You want my opinion?"

I wanted to say no, but my head nodded involuntarily.

"He didn't drown."

"You're saying my father's dead? He's definitely dead?"

Ripping a second slice out of the pizza box, he nodded. "I don't like to make things up, so I'll tell you. Yeah. He's dead."

There was a resounding knock, then the door swung wide a third time. A young woman entered, also in a white lab coat. "Fire in the Quarter," she said. "Police expect one, maybe more. They're saying arson."

My nerves jangled. *Arson?*

The coroner shook his head. "So supper'll have to wait."

He tapped his chubby fingers on the refrigerated cabinets, counting five over from the right side and three down, and jerked the drawer open. I expected to see a body inside. Instead, the drawer was filled with food and condiments. Two pickle jars, milk, yogurt, a bag of seedless grapes. He closed the lid of the pizza box and slid it and the sandwich into the drawer with the other food.

I took Ronny by the arm. He opened his eyes. He had the look of someone trying not to throw up.

We left through the door we had come in.

◄ SEVENTEEN ►

The Running Begins

I tried hard not to think the worst — *arson!* — but by the time we got home, fire engines, police cruisers, ambulances, and television vans were everywhere. Streets had been cordoned off. The air was gray with falling ash and clouds of dark smoke. My heart iced when I saw the flames.

"Our house," I said. "Ronny! Our house!"

His face was dark. "Uncle Carl?" he said quietly. "Was he there?"

"What? No. He was away. He went away this morning. Our house! Oh, man —"

"Then who was the coroner lady talking about?" Ronny asked. "Did someone really die?"

I looked at him. "We can ask —"

"No," he said. "Don't let on that it's our house."

I couldn't do anything but watch the flames exploding out the front windows and reaching up toward the roof. The *faux chambre* was untouched so far, wrapped in thick scarves of smoke, but for how long? Flames spilled higher by the minute. Sirens shrieked close, then stopped. We pushed in as far as we could. Firefighters hosed the walls through the blasted windows. My eyes kept going back to the fake room. Why? What was there? Trains? Books?

"Do you hear them?" Ronny asked.

I listened. Over the sound of the roaring flames and water, I heard voices. "Yes."

"Cane did this," he went on. "You know he did. He found out where we live. He knows all about us. Wait here."

Ronny pushed through the crowd to a man wearing a tie and jacket, standing in the middle of a circle of cops. As he did, a shape moved up behind me in the darkness. I jumped.

"It's just me, Derek Stone."

I turned to see Big Bob Lemon, hunched over and staring up at the flames. He seemed smaller than the last time I'd seen him.

"Sorry about your home," he said in his low, rumbling voice.

I had to say it.

"You were there, weren't you?"

He turned his head, looked down at me.

"You were there in 1938, on that train that crashed into the Gap. You were nine, hiding out on that train. Weren't you?"

Lemon glanced over at Ronny, who was out of ear-shot. He nodded. "I was hiding out, yes. Boys did that then. I saw things happen that night. I dismissed them a long time ago, until your brother showed up and reminded me what I saw."

I knew it.

"You saw people die then, who are back now," I said.

Lemon nodded. "The dead are back. I knew it when that boy there came to me. He said things that proved he was the one who saved my life that day so long ago. He's that kind of boy."

I blinked. The ashes stung my eyes. "So Virgil was an okay guy? He's not like Cane at all?"

"Virgil Black was just a young man who happened to have a really bad first day of work. But the others who came back from that first crash? Murderers and arsonists. They found some way from their world to ours. A rift. And I'm talking rift with a capital R."

The Rift, I thought. The word took my breath away. It sounded horrific. But it explained it perfectly.

"Can it be closed?" I asked. "Can the Rift be closed?"

"Does a tear in a cloth ever become smaller?" he said darkly. "No, the road to the afterlife — it's a two-way street. How many dead have you seen so far?"

I thought about Cane and the other soldier. I believed that the woman at the coffee shop was Abby Donner's mother. The man who was with her was probably dead, too. "Five," I said. "Including Ronny."

"So far," Lemon added. "That leaves your daddy and three others we don't know about."

Ronny returned then, saw Bob Lemon, and nodded. "Somebody spotted a guy with a crew cut. They have some cars out looking for him. It was Cane."

"But what does he want?" I asked.

"To win," Ronny said.

"To win?" I said, glancing at Lemon. "What does that mean? Win what?"

"All of this. Here. The world. We're at war," Ronny said.

I looked into his face. "What?" I didn't — couldn't — understand.

"We're at war, the evil ones and us. We have been for ages. That's what's been eating at me since we went back to the Gap. There's a war, and it's been going on for centuries, and I'm a soldier in it. Only now, the war is spilling up here."

"But what about me? Why do they want me?" I asked.

"I don't know," he said. "I don't —"

Boooom! The second floor of my house burst into

flames now, and the police pushed the crowd farther back.

"I'm getting out of here now," Lemon said. "You should, too." His face was grim. He probably thought we wouldn't make it. Maybe he thought nobody would. Looking around nervously, he hustled off.

Ronny swung around on his heels. He tilted his head. "Cane!" he whispered. "He's still here. We have to bolt. Now!"

Ronny wrapped his cold hand around my arm and pulled. His grip was freezing. We ran down the sidewalks between houses, him pulling, me stumbling after. The voices surged again.

"They sense us near," Ronny said.

I looked back. Through the crowd I spotted the giant man and his wiry friend as if they were the only ones there. Cane's face was like the front of a truck. His arms were bowed as if his muscles were too big to allow them to hang properly. He was two hundred and fifty pounds of dead, running at us.

And there were three others with them this time, one of them a woman.

"Come on," said Ronny. *"Come on!"*

As we slid into an alley and flickered past the dark windows, the voices grew louder, wilder in my ear.

I ran as fast as my chunky legs would carry me.

⊣ EIGHTEEN ⊢

Public Transportation

"**W**here are we going?" I huffed. "We have no place to go!"

"In here," Ronny said when we reached the edge of the Quarter. We ducked into a narrow alley between two buildings. It was jammed with garbage cans. A large trash container loomed at the far end. The pavement was wet, blackly reflecting the facades on both sides.

I hurried on, cursing the fact that I was so overweight. Ronny let my arm go and shot ahead into the dark. He squeezed past the container and was gone.

I stopped. "Ronny?"

No sound now, except for sudden heavy breathing. It was my own chest sucking in, blowing out.

I ran to the trash container and leaned around it. No Ronny. Where had he gone? The lamppost above flashed on, then off, then flickered quickly, as if huge amounts of electricity were flooding through the wires. I couldn't see. Where had Ronny gone? My stubby fingers shook like dry leaves.

"Ronny!" I yelled.

The alley ahead was strangely quiet. All sound had been sucked out of the air except the far-away strain of a lone trumpet. It echoed from a few streets over.

My chest trembled hot and cold. I thought I would vomit. I walked down the alley, turned a corner. Decatur Street flashed neon blue, orange, blue, orange. I felt sicker by the minute.

Then Ronny was behind me. His grip on my arm was sudden, cold. "This way."

"Where were you?" I asked.

"This way," he said again. His face was iron, white, immobile, his eyes fixed on another cluster of trash cans at the far end of the alley. He walked toward them, then slowed.

"What is it?" I whispered, seeing nothing.

Ronny didn't speak.

I looked again. A shape rose slowly against the light, glowing blue, then orange, then blue again. It was the giant with the crew cut, a massive shape as dark as night, rising. In profile at first, his head turned to us. He grinned.

"Get out of here!" said Ronny, pushing me back.

But I couldn't. I couldn't. Three more shapes appeared and backed us against the trash cans. I tried to climb onto one of the cans, but it rolled, and I fell.

Out of nowhere, the wiry man leaped at Ronny, making a crazy noise in his throat. Two more shapes joined in. The one in the front was the train conductor, his uniform in tatters, his eyes sick and yellow. One sleeve dangled loosely. He had lost an arm in the wreck. It didn't slow him down.

Ronny fell to the street. The wiry man tumbled with him. Ronny leaped up and scuttled past the conductor. Cane watched with dead, black eyes.

I threw myself at the third attacker from behind. He was another passenger from the train, a gray-haired man. I didn't know what I was doing, but I moved as quickly as I could. The man tripped and went down. He growled a horrible noise, then tried to get to his feet, his head twisting up at me.

I surprised myself by stamping hard on his back. The man scraped his knees, shred his pants on the pavement, and fell flat again. He groaned, then laughed as if possessed. "Ha! Ha!" The sound was unearthly.

The woman was there now. Abby Donner's mother. She ran at us.

"Ladder!" Ronny yelled, pushing me toward a wall ladder glinting in the alley light. "Get up there!"

I struggled up the wet rungs to the rooftop, with Ronny an instant behind me. The roof was flat, bordered by a high wall in the rear. A rusty door stood in the wall.

"The roof!" came a screech from below. It was the one-armed conductor. The ladder rungs squealed as two, three sets of leather soles climbed up. Cane was not among them. *What is he waiting for?*

I yanked open the door. Ronny and I plunged inside the building. It was dark. He rummaged a pipe from a pile of scrap and slid it through the handle, past the inside of the door frame.

Almost instantly, we heard banging on the outside of the door.

"Hurry," Ronny said. We crept along a railed balcony on an inside wall overlooking an array of ugly machines, table saws, cartons, forklifts, sacks of grain or sand. We found a door, jerked it open onto a street opposite the alley, and raced out.

The woman and the gray-haired dead man were waiting for us.

"How —" I started.

Ronny faked a lunge at them, pushing me back through the door onto the floor and slamming it behind him. "Ronny!" I yelled.

The noises from outside were awful, inhuman, like animals at a kill. I heard a wild cry, then footsteps stuttering away into the night. I tore the door open. The alley was empty. They were all gone. So was Ronny.

I slumped to the ground, nearly sobbing. Ronny had drawn the dead away from me. But was he quick enough to get away from them?

The pavement gleamed in purple neon. I heard a police siren, two, three, in conflicting rhythm in the distance, all closing in. Had someone seen us fighting? Could the police help me?

There was a crash of glass, crystals sprinkling the ground, then the sound of heavy footsteps.

I spun around. A lone man walked toward me slowly, his sausage arms pumping like pistons. Erskine Cane.

This was what he had been waiting for.

I ran north into the streets around the park. I kept running. Cane's footsteps followed me relentlessly. The sirens were only a distant wail now, crisscrossing the sound of the dead. Was someone there? Anyone?

I was in a part of town I didn't know. A maze of dark streets. I should have stayed in the Quarter. Never mind. Cane was near, and I had nothing to fight with but my hands. Fat hands. Stubby fingers.

The voices in my head were deafening now. Growling. Shouting. Cane moved along the pavement toward me. I burst out of an alley and saw a streetcar rumbling along on its tracks. Yes! If it stopped, people might get off. I could mix with them, get lost in the crowd.

Maybe.

If it didn't stop, I might be able to run fast enough to climb on. Would it be crowded? Cane wouldn't do anything with people around. Would he?

I had to try.

My thick legs hustled toward the rolling car. The streetcar wasn't slowing. Cane hurried after me with loping steps, increasing strides. I kept running, pushing a teenage couple out of the way. They yelled after me. The car shuttled along more quickly than I expected. I wasn't going to make it. Cane was ten paces behind me. Eight. I faltered.

A white hand suddenly reached out from the crowded streetcar. It slapped onto my arm. I screamed like an idiot.

"Jump for it!" called a voice. "Derek — jump for it!"

I looked up. My heart nearly exploded.

I was looking into the face of my father.

◄ NINETEEN ►

The Hand

He pulled me onto the streetcar with one hand.

"Dad!" I cried. People stared as I tumbled to the streetcar's floor. "Dad! Dad!" It was like I was struck dumb except for that one word. "Dad!" I wrapped my arms around him. "Dad —"

He stiffened and pushed me away. I saw his eyes — tired, hard — scan the receding street.

Cane was nowhere in sight.

My father was huddled and filthy. His beard looked a month old. His shirt was ripped and ill-fitting. The raincoat on his back was stained, shabby, and not his. These weren't the clothes he had worn on the train with Ronny and me.

"How did you — where were you —"

"Quiet!" he said, squeezing my arm like a vise. I tried to see both of his hands. The car was too crowded. I couldn't.

"Ronny is alive!" I blurted out, then hushed myself. "Ronny is here. Everyone thinks you're dead —"

More people looked.

"Shhh!" he hissed. "Listen —"

"But, Dad —"

"Listen to me!" he snapped. "I know about Ronny. We can't talk now. They're everywhere. More than you think —"

"More?"

Dad scanned the passengers quickly, squinting in the gray light of the streetcar's lamps.

I wouldn't let go of him. "I can't believe you're back —"

"There are dozens of them all over," he continued. "I have to hide. Look, I saw something happen in that ravine. The river, it . . . opened . . ."

I saw the water, too, felt it surround me — then shook it off. "I know," I said. "Ronny told me the same thing. Only he's not . . . he's not Ronny."

Dad's eyes searched my face for a second. "There's a way to close it. I think there is. It's . . . complicated. But before we can do anything, I have to go —"

"Go? No, Dad, you can't leave me again —"

He shook off my hand, raised his own hand to his forehead and massaged it, over and over. His eyes scanned the other streetcar passengers.

"There's no choice," he grunted, pulling me toward the rear of the car. "This is dangerous."

"Everything okay back there?" hollered the conductor, watching us in the rearview mirror.

"Oh, shut . . . yes! Fine," my father shouted. He was annoyed, angry. "Everything's fine." He drew me closer, shifting his gaze to the streets again. "Go to the cemetery. To the old tomb. The original one."

"The original . . ." I wasn't sure what he meant.

"The Longtemps tomb," he said.

"Mom's family? Why that one?"

"There's a message there," Dad snapped. "About where to meet me. I can't tell you more. Not here. We need to split up now."

I couldn't leave yet. I had to know.

"How did you survive the crash?" I asked.

The streetlights flickered blue, green, amber in his eyes as we passed the late-night music clubs. The car traveled slowly, but Dad's head was swiveling around like a crazed searchlight. It reminded me of what the short man did at the ravine.

"You didn't fall into the river, did you?" I pressed.

"I can't tell you now," he said. "I don't know. I don't remember that. The fall was . . . I don't know."

He was struggling with words. It was hard to watch his face contort. He was so different. Dad had changed so much from that day at TrainMania. His face twitched with fear. I tried again to see his hands, but he kept one buried in his raincoat pocket. Remembering the coroner's plastic container made my stomach roll over.

"The dead are walking again," Dad whispered. "They're coming together. It's horrible. But you — you saw something, Derek —"

"Me?"

"You saw something that night ten years ago in the bayou, and you need to remember it."

"Dad, no. What?"

He took my chin in his hand and stared into my eyes. "The girl," he said. "If she wakes up, you have to find her."

"What girl?" I said. "Dad, this is crazy. You mean Abby? The coma girl?"

"The girl from the train. If she wakes up, you have to get to her. Find her. Find . . ."

The car slowed. Some passengers climbed down onto the street, oblivious to the terror in their midst. At the same time, three people hopped into the front of the streetcar.

After the car started up, I shifted on my feet, trying to get a glimpse of them. My knees weakened.

My ears rang with voices.

One was the wiry man. Another was the woman from the alley, Abby Donner's mother. The third was a tall man with his head bowed. He turned to me. Cane. His lips curled into that mad smile.

My chest went ice cold. "Dad —"

"So, you can sense them," Dad said to me, following my gaze. "You can use that."

He stepped toward Cane.

"You can't fight him, Dad," I said. "He's a killer. He's got weapons —"

Trapped by traffic, the car lurched to a halt, and Cane rushed at us. My father swung me behind him and pushed. I nearly toppled an old woman.

The next seconds were a blur.

Something flashed in the dim light, sliding sharply down the silver hand pole. The sound of ripping cloth echoed in my bad ear.

"Ahh!" My father sucked in a huge breath.

A woman screamed. "He stabbed that man!" she cried, pointing at Cane. "He stabbed him!"

"Dad!" I cried. Cane's arm went low and started up toward Dad's chest. I kicked the giant's kneecap, and he fell back slightly.

"Get off me, you!" said an older man, pushing Cane from behind.

A shape hustled over from the far end of the car. I cowered. We couldn't fight off another one. We couldn't.

But it was Big Bob Lemon, his teeth set in anger. How he got there, I can't tell you. He hurled himself at Cane — the eighty-year-old guy did this! — knocking the dark hulk backward. Cane hit the floor of the car, taking three people down with him. Everyone was shouting, screaming.

The conductor set off an alarm. "I'm alerting the police!"

My father hung back, hunched over, still.

I thrust a man aside to get to Dad, but a strong hand took my shoulder from behind. Who did that? The conductor kept blowing his whistle, and I heard a police siren *whoop* through traffic nearby.

My father swung toward me. "Derek, you know something that will stop them. Keep it safe —"

"What?" I said. "What are you talking about?"

He struggled to say something — or *not* say something. "You were always smart, Derek. Be smart now —"

Cane was on his feet again. He reached out with one of his piston arms and ripped me away from my father. He dragged me to the front of the car and pushed the conductor into the street. The car jerked forward. Cane's fingers were like an iron vise, crushing my arm as he pulled my face to his. The hollow eyes, the black teeth — he reeked of death.

I screamed like a baby. It felt as if the bones in my shoulder would snap. I sank to my knees.

My father and Lemon ran forward, battering Cane's grip again and again until I was free. I tried to stand, but my knees buckled and my left foot slipped off the streetcar's deck. I grabbed wildly for the handrail, but missed.

"Dad —" I yelled.

"Go where I told you!" he shouted back at me.

I tumbled into the street as the car hurtled onward. Police converged on it.

I ran the other way, pushing through crowds, still feeling the giant's cold grip on my shoulder. I pushed through the midnight crowds until I found a deserted alley between two busy streets. I slumped to the ground, breathless and sick.

For minutes, I didn't move. My ears burned.

I tried to understand it all, then gave that up and began to cry. It was too much. It had to end. I wouldn't be able to take it.

But I had to take it. I had to.

My father was alive!

It gnawed at me that I hadn't seen his other hand. It sounds terrible, but I wanted to see blood. I wanted to know that, as banged-up as he was, Dad had somehow made it out of the ravine alive. That he wasn't like the others. That he wasn't like Ronny. His clothes were wrinkled, wet. His face was cut and scratched. He had a gash on his forehead. But it was night. The lights from the street, the shops, the restaurants, were garish. Was he bleeding? I couldn't tell. I couldn't tell!

I needed to find Ronny. Where was he?

Never mind that now. No. I had to go to the old tomb. The very thought made me shiver. The tomb was in the most ancient section of St. Louis Cemetery, in the oldest neighborhood of the City of the Dead, where not even workers dared go after the sun went down. That was where my father was sending me.

I had to go.

◄| TWENTY |►

Run. Run.

The night air was close and wet as I approached the oldest part of the oldest boneyard. Its tombs stood silent, row upon row, like a derelict city, long abandoned by the living.

As I searched for a way over the wrought-iron fence, an old joke came back to me.

Why do cemeteries have fences around them?

Because people are dying to get in.

Only the opposite was true. People were dying to get *out*. According to Ronny, to my father, to Big Bob Lemon, to everyone, they were all dying to get out.

And they weren't coming to haunt us. They were a gathering army of the dead, and they wanted us dead, too.

Dead, or worse.

I thought I heard a sound. I turned, and saw headlights. Pickup trucks, two of them, circled the cemetery from different directions. I almost wished they were after me. Real people in real trucks. Not the dead.

My blood froze from my forehead on down. Dad said I know something? I saw something? What do I know? What did I see?

Never mind. I had to move. I found a loose gate and squeezed between it and its iron frame. I scratched my shoulder and knee, but didn't stop to look. My knee stung, and it felt good.

Once inside, I took a moment to get my bearings. *The old tomb*, he'd said.

Not the tomb where the memorial was, but the Longtemps tomb. The tomb of my mother's family. What did *she* have to do with this? Why *her* family's tomb? She hadn't been around for ten years. She didn't even know that Ronny was . . .

Never mind. Focus. Find the tomb.

I wound through the narrow cemetery streets. I'd been to the old tomb only once before, a few days before my mother left.

I remembered it now.

It was a rainy morning, gray. The graveyard streets were puddled with black water. I told my mother I was afraid of water. But she took my arm and led me to the tomb. She talked. She said things.

What things?

She knelt to me, crying as she held my shoulders and kissed me.

Why? What did she say?

And suddenly the memories faded because I found it.

A tall, narrow house made of alabaster but blackened by grime, the Longtemps tomb shone yellow under a flickering streetlamp. On the curb in front of it lay a loose bunch of flowers.

My knees dampened through my pants when I knelt to the gravel. I heard a lone trumpet three or four cemetery streets over. It was late for a mourner.

Bah-dep! Dep!

A sudden footstep. I rose into a crouch, prepared to run.

"It's me," said Ronny, appearing beside me.

"Where have you been —"

"Who left the flowers?" he asked without emotion.

I read the card. One word: *Bonton.*

"Bonton?" said Ronny.

"It's Cajun slang for 'good times,'" I said. "You know that." No, I had to remind myself. *Ronny* knows that.

I felt like sobbing. Burning-hot air heaved up from my lungs. This wasn't going to stop, was it? The insanity was growing around me. It moved closer, took over every normal thing in my life. Up wasn't up anymore. Down wasn't down.

Dead Ronny. Maybe not-dead Dad. Big Bob Lemon. A piece of knuckle in a sandwich box. The false room. Daddy Jubal. Angola Freight. Erskine Cane. Virgil Black. Abby Donner, the coma girl!

Is this my life now?

"I remember him," said Ronny slowly. "There was a guy named Bonton. Bonton Fouks."

"When? In 1938? In Shongaloo?"

"Bonton Smitty Fouks," he said again. "No, he was a friend of your . . . of Dad's."

I stood up, blood rushing to my head. "You remember that? I mean, the Ronny stuff is still there? Are you . . . coming back?"

He growled. "Shut up. I don't know. It's a mess in here. All I know is there was a guy named Bonton Fouks who lived in a place called Bayou Malpierre."

Bayou Malpierre.

"Are you kidding me?" I said.

The nightmare rushed over me — I couldn't breathe, couldn't move, and the dogs were after me again.

I sucked in as big a breath of air as I could, but I couldn't fill my lungs. "I don't like bayous."

"Well, I don't like people cutting me up, either!" he

snapped. "Or hunting your poppa or burning your house or trying to take you —"

"Take me?"

"You can't be here alone."

"So where have you been for the last few hours?"

"Don't . . . don't ask me that," Ronny said. "Just don't. I don't know how to tell you what it is, or *where* it is, and you wouldn't want to know. But I'll help you."

I looked into his face, twisted in pain. "How?"

"I'll help you find your father . . . *our* father," he said with a kind of shrug. "I want to go back. I want to rest with my family again. On the other side. I don't like it here, but I . . . I can't leave you alone. Maybe I can remember things. Maybe I can protect you. I'll try."

Somehow, that made me more sad than glad. I needed him. But the fact that he *knew* I needed him, that I couldn't get on without him — a dead person I didn't really know! — made me feel like giving up.

"It's a clue," Ronny said, extending his hand. "We need to go to the bayou. Come on."

I looked toward the city beyond the fence. I saw the night oozing through its streets. I wanted to see the sun creep up out of the dark and illuminate the world, dry everything up. But the sun was so far away. It seemed farther away every second. I was living in the dark now.

A noise sounded, only it wasn't a trumpet this time. It was the squeal of a gate on the far side of the cemetery.

Then, with a sudden intake of breath as if the whole city paused to listen, there came the *thud, thud, thud* of shoes pounding and twisting the cemetery gravel.

Ronny's eyes were wild. "Them."

I saw the moving shapes in the distance. Five. Six. Seven.

I knew then what I hadn't been able to believe before. The dead really *were* after me. They wanted me. But why? *Why?*

Ronny nodded toward the fence. "We've got to go. Bayou Malpierre."

I took his hand. It was cold, a grip of death, but it was tight against my palm. He pulled. I followed.

With the sound of footsteps closing in behind us, we ducked between the tombs, hoisted ourselves over the fence, and made for the open streets.

We ran.

T·H·E
HAUNTING
of
Derek Stone

Don't miss the next volume in Derek's story...

BAYOU DOGS

Turn the page for a special sneak peek!

THE HAUNTING of Derek Stone

BAYOU DOGS

The night streets slithered in front of us like dark snakes. They urged us every wrong way, crisscrossed one another, coiled back on themselves, stopped abruptly.

My brother Ronny wasn't having any of it. He kept running straight, feet slapping the wet pavement. His hand gripped mine, dragging me forward.

Like madmen fleeing their shadows, my mind told me, *or the shadows of others.*

Like so many times before, I had no time to wonder where those words came from. I just ran — past houses, shops, restaurants, through crowded alleys — the whole noisy mess of the French Quarter at night.

My footsteps pounded the ground, jarred my bones. I tried to dodge the puddles as I ran. No luck. I barreled on and hoped I wouldn't fall on my face. I couldn't slow down. I couldn't rest. I couldn't stop.

"This way," Ronny said. "Hurry up!"

"I'm hurrying," I said, gasping for air.

"Not fast enough!" he snarled. "They're gaining on us."

I already knew that.

We'd been racing through the streets for over an hour in the dead of night. We still couldn't shake them. No matter where we ran, the low voices pierced my ear, whispering, hissing, growling a mile behind us, half a mile, getting closer. Horrible voices.

Their voices.

They used to be people, but they weren't people anymore.

They were the dead. And now they were back.

The shadows of others, my mind said again. I shook my head. There were a lot of things I didn't understand rattling around up there.

"Behind us and to our left," Ronny said. "Five minutes at most. I hear them calling each other."

I nodded. "So do I —"

"Well, thanks to you, we can't outrun them," he snapped, throwing down my hand. "We have to hide. Follow me."

Ronny was angry, but he was right. I was out of shape. I did slow us down.

He turned abruptly on his heel and entered a side street. It was darker there. Two of the three street lamps were out. The third flickered. Ronny scanned the houses on both sides of the street, looking for a vacant one. I watched his eyes dart back and forth, grateful for the chance to stop running. My lungs burned, my throat ached, my knees quaked under me.

I was fat. I was scared. Life was speeding up. Everything around me was spinning. I hated it. School, friends, family, home — everything I knew — was gone.

"Keep it down a little," Ronny said. "You're moaning again."

Maybe I was. You'd be moaning, too, if you were in my shoes. But don't worry. You might be, soon enough.

Ronny turned his head slowly from side to side, then twitched suddenly. He took a short step toward one dark house, paused, took another step.

"That one's empty," he whispered. "Come on . . ."

He loped down the narrow side yard and up a set of wooden steps. He forced open the back door with a quick thrust of his arm. There was a splintering crack.

Ronny grabbed the door to stifle the noise.

"In," he said.

Stale air, thick with the smell of mold, breathed out at me from the opening. It smelled like the house was gasping its last.

"It stinks," I said.

"Cover your nose," he hissed. "Do you want them to find you?" Pushing me inside, he looked out at the street one last time and quickly shut the door behind us.

Ronny was right about the house being empty. It had the sullen, hollow feeling of abandonment. Even the furniture was gone. I collapsed breathless on the floor. The boards were soggy and rotten. Rain had poured in through a busted window and puddled on the floor. My pants soaked through when I sat down. I didn't bother to get up. I couldn't. I didn't care.

"Ronny —" I started.

"Quiet. They're less than a mile away. They'll hear you."

He was right about that, too.

The dead were coming. They were coming for me.

My name is Derek Stone. I'm fourteen. And I'll try to make it as simple as possible for you to understand. The dead have come back.

Impossible, right?

Yeah, I wish. If you want the s[...]
began a few weeks ago when a trai[...]
brother, my father, and me crashed into[...]
called Bordelon Gap. Nine passengers[...]
was lucky. I survived.

Ronny wasn't so lucky. He died.

Sort of.

It's complicated.

I'd discovered the hard way about a thing called *translation*. My term. At the very moment of death, when a soul flees its dying body, another soul — one that's been dead for a long time — can take its place and reanimate that body.

How do I know? I know.

Ronny jerked away from the window and walked from room to room, obviously searching for something. I was about to ask him what, when he came back with a beat-up broom in his hands.

"Going to clean up?" I asked.

Ronny snapped the long handle over his knee and tossed away the bristled half. Then swung the three-foot, jagged-tipped stake in the air. "I'll clean up. If I'm lucky."

He scowled and took his position at the front window again. When he did things like this, I wasn't talking to my brother. I was talking to the country boy who had become a fighter.

what Virgil remembered about his seventy
s in the land of the dead before he came back in
'onny's body, a war between good and evil has gone
on for centuries. And guess what? Things weren't
going so well for the good guys. They were completely outnumbered by dark souls who wanted to
annihilate them.

When the fabric tore and the Rift opened, the evil
dead realized they could spread their war among the
living.

So they came back.

I know. I don't want to believe it, either.

"Why are they taking so long?" Ronny wondered
aloud, moving from window to window.

I checked my watch. We'd been running and hiding for nearly two hours already, but as close as
the dead sounded at times, they weren't. The voices
closed in, then coiled away, then came in again. It
sounded like they were circling away and back like
waves in a tide.

"You're moaning again," said Ronny, his eyes flash-
ing at me.

"Sorry," I said.

"Just keep it down."

Ronny parted the curtains carefully and looked
out. I did, too. The only streetlamp with a glimmer

of life shone dull brown and then sick yellow on the glazed pavement. Nothing. Not yet.

"Do you think we should move on?" I whispered.

"To where? To your house?" Ronny said. "Think about it."

I felt like saying, "You start," but kept my mouth shut. Since he died, Ronny had no sense of humor.

But he was right about my house. Erskine Cane had torched it just hours before. Why, I'm not sure. But Cane was after me. I knew that for certain.

"Ronny," I started, "about Cane —"

All of a sudden, my cell phone rang.

"Turn that thing off!" Ronny snapped.

"Sorry," I said.

I opened the phone and noticed that I had only two battery bars left. It was Uncle Carl calling. He had been living with us since the crash. He'd been in Oregon on a business trip when our house burned down, but he'd just now heard about the fire. He was crazy with worry.

"The alarm company finally tracked me down!" Carl yelled in my ear. "There was a break-in at the house? Then a fire? Are you boys okay? What's going on?"

A break-in? I didn't know that part. I lied and told Carl that we were spending the night at my friend

Tooley's house. Ronny and I would be meeting with the fire marshal in the morning. I lied and lied. I didn't know exactly what we were doing, but I knew we couldn't stay put. Carl was smart, but easy to fool. He trusted me. I felt like a criminal.

Right. Me, a criminal. Chubby boy, Derek Stone. Me, running for my life from dead people. *I'm* the criminal!

"So you're both all right?" Carl asked, clearly relieved. I told him we were. "I'm coming right home, anyway," he said. "I'll be back there later today."

"We'll see you tonight at Tooley's house," I lied. I had no idea where we'd be tonight. If we'd be anywhere at all.

Carl said he would let the police know that we were fine. We hung up, and I tucked my phone in my pocket.

"Try to keep that off until we need it," said Ronny, stalking quietly from window to window as if he'd done this sort of thing before.

Ronny tensed at the window.

I went to him. "What is it?" I whispered.

Peering between a pair of filthy curtains, I spied a shadow moving in and out of the light. It was a figure, tall and thick. "Oh, no, no, no . . ."

"Quiet," Ronny said.

"Can you see his face? Is it —"

"Quiet!" he snapped.

The figure moved out of view. I cocked my bad ear. Why were the voices so quiet? I turned my head. Where were they?

For minutes, we didn't move.

Then there was a click at the back door.

I heard the door swing open and tap against the inside wall of the kitchen. I couldn't breathe. My lungs burned. My heart hammered. I looked for a weapon, picked up the other half of Ronny's broom, and held it out like a bayonet.

Footsteps sounded heavily on the floorboards. Ronny crept behind the door, his pointed broom handle aimed high.

Thunk . . . thunk . . .

The door flew open.

Discover the world on the other side of night...

Meet

OLIVER
NOCTURNE

He's not your
typical vampire.

#1: THE
VAMPIRE'S
PHOTOGRAPH

Oliver Nocturne has a fairly typical childhood—for
a vampire. But Oliver is different from those around
him—his gore-loving vampire schoolmates, his macabre
vampire parents, and his obnoxious older brother, Bane.
That's because, unbeknownst to Oliver, he's a little more
human than the rest of them. He becomes even more
drawn into the human world when Emalie, a headstrong
girl with a troubled past, manages to take a picture of
him. Soon he is trying to uncover the truth about his
origins and his special purpose in the vampire world.

OLIVER NOCTURNE

#2: THE SUNLIGHT SLAYINGS

Oliver is convinced that he's lost the only real friends he's ever had—Emalie and Dean. But then Dean turns up, still dead but now a zombie, and apparently he isn't holding any grudges. Who brought Dean back—and why? And what is going on with Emalie—could she be behind the magical slayings of several young vampires? Oliver and Dean must discover the truth before Oliver himself winds up turned to dust.